Sierra Carlton was the very last woman with whom he should be spending time.

Yet here he was. Again. She was getting to be a bad habit that he couldn't seem to control. Yet, the evenings that he and the girls didn't spend here with Sierra and her daughter, Tyree, seemed strangely flat and incomplete now.

He tried to think of her as his business partner, maybe even a friend. Instead he kept dreaming about putting his hands on her, laying his mouth against the long, graceful column of her throat.

Oh, man. What was he doing? And why couldn't he stop?

Dear Reader,

It's that time of year again—when every woman's thoughts turn to love—and we have all kinds of romantic gifts for you! We begin with the latest from reader favorite Allison Leigh, *Secretly Married,* in which she concludes her popular TURNABOUT miniseries. A woman who was sure she was divorced finds out there's the little matter of her not-so-ex-husband's signing the papers, so off she goes to Turnabout—the island that can turn your life around—to get her divorce. Or does she?

Our gripping MERLYN COUNTY MIDWIVES miniseries continues with Gina Wilkins's *Countdown to Baby.* A woman interested only in baby-making—or so she thinks—may be finding happily-ever-after *and* her little bundle of joy, with the town's most eligible bachelor. LOGAN'S LEGACY, our new Silhouette continuity, is introduced in *The Virgin's Makeover* by Judy Duarte, in which a plain-Jane adoptee is transformed in time to find her inner beauty…and, just possibly, her biological family. Look for the next installment in this series coming next month. Shirley Hailstock's *Love on Call* tells the story of two secretive emergency-room doctors who find temptation—not to mention danger—in each other. In *Down from the Mountain* by Barbara Gale, two disabled people—a woman without sight, and a scarred man—nonetheless find each other a perfect match. And Arlene James continues THE RICHEST GALS IN TEXAS with *Fortune Finds Florist.* A sudden windfall turns complicated when a wealthy small-town florist forms a business relationship—for starters—with a younger man who has more than finance on his mind.

So Happy Valentine's Day, and don't forget to join us next month, for six special romances, all from Silhouette Special Edition.

Sincerely,

Gail Chasan
Senior Editor

Please address questions and book requests to:
Silhouette Reader Service
U.S.: 3010 Walden Ave., P.O. Box 1325, Buffalo, NY 14269
Canadian: P.O. Box 609, Fort Erie, Ont. L2A 5X3

Fortune Finds Florist

ARLENE JAMES

SPECIAL EDITION®

Published by Silhouette Books

America's Publisher of Contemporary Romance

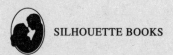 **SILHOUETTE BOOKS**

ISBN 0-373-24596-3

FORTUNE FINDS FLORIST

Books by Arlene James

ARLENE JAMES

grew up in Oklahoma and has lived all over the South. In 1976 she married "the most romantic man in the world." The author enjoys traveling with her husband, but writing has always been her chief pastime. Arlene is also the author of the inspirational titles *Proud Spirit, A Wish for Always, Partners for Life* and *No Stranger to Love.*

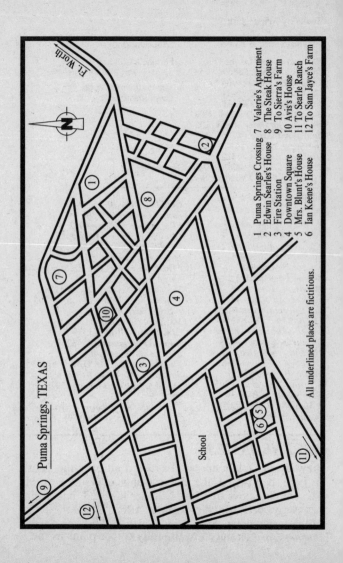

Puma Springs, TEXAS

N

Ft. Worth

1 Puma Springs Crossing
2 Edwin Searles's House
3 Fire Station
4 Downtown Square
5 Mrs. Blunt's House
6 Ian Keene's House
7 Valerie's Apartment
8 The Steak House
9 To Sierra's Farm
10 Avis's House
11 To Searle Ranch
12 To Sam Jayce's Farm

School

All underlined places are fictitious.

Chapter One

Sam shined the toes of his boots on the backs of the legs of his starched, dark blue jeans and tugged at the open collar of his freshly ironed, maroon-plaid shirt. Smoothing the sides of the boxy cattleman's coat that he wore for protection against the cold north wind, he sucked in one more deep breath. He was as ready as he was ever going to be.

It felt odd preparing to talk business with a woman. Farming was usually a man's province, but like he'd told the banker who'd put him onto this setup, "The times they were a-changing, and a wise man realized when he couldn't stand against a tide." Besides, he'd done his research, and Sam wasn't as convinced of the folly of her plans as the bankers were. Farming flowers might be unusual in West Central Texas, but it was entirely possible, provided a man—or woman—had access to all the necessary resources. He did not, but neither did Sierra Carlton. Together…ah, now *that* was another proposition altogether, and one he'd come prepared to make. Couldn't be all that different than talking his way into an equipment loan.

Sam looked up at the crisp brick front of the Lorimer building. Like Sierra Carlton, Avis Lorimer was one of the famed Puma Springs heiresses. They, along with a third woman named Valerie Keene, had each inherited a cool million from an old man whom everyone around town had assumed was a pauper, including the old man's nephew, Heston Witt, who just happened to be mayor, a position ripe for embarrassment when people learned he had pretty much gotten left out of the will. Heston's nose had been out of joint since because of it, much to the amusement of most of the town, although that didn't stop anyone from repeating the gossip he spouted.

Sam didn't have the foggiest idea what Valerie Keene had done with her money. All he knew about her was that she was rumored to have been quite the party girl before she married the town's fire marshal.

He'd heard worse about Avis Lorimer. Some said she was a home wrecker and possibly even a "widow-on-purpose," but she'd stepped in and used her money to erect this fine new building on the Puma Springs town square after the old one had burned and left an ugly, gaping hole in the block.

As for Sierra Carlton, it was rumored that she was the disinherited child of a wealthy Fort Worth businessman. Some said she was divorced, and some said she had never been married, though she had a daughter. Sam, however, was the last man to judge another. God knew that he lived with his own enduring scandal.

Sam pushed open the heavy glass door to the florist's shop and stepped inside to the sound of muted chimes. Warmth and a wave of flowery perfume washed over him. He glanced around the large, attractively arrayed showroom. A moment later a short, heavy woman with a mannish haircut appeared from a doorway on the right. Assuming that she was Sierra Carlton, he introduced himself.

"I'm Sam Jayce."

"Pleased to meet you, Mr. Jayce. I'm Bette Grouper. How can I help you?"

"Oh. Uh, I have an appointment with Ms. Carlton."

The wide woman motioned to a flight of stairs on the left. "It's at the front of the building. Just knock and go on in."

Feeling foolish, Sam nodded his thanks and moved to the staircase. He started climbing. About halfway up, he paused, wiped his palms on his thighs and checked his hair with both hands. He'd been cursed with a cowlick right in front, so he'd taken to spiking his short, thick hair, not that it needed much help to stand up on end. Frowning, he dropped his hands and took the remainder of the stairs two at a time, keenly aware that if he'd been meeting with a man he'd have just worn a cap and said to hell with it. Dealing with females—adult females, anyway—always changed the equation, and that woman downstairs had unnerved him. For a moment he'd thought he was going to be doing business with someone who put him in mind of his grandma. That could still happen.

At the top of the stairs he turned left, toward the front of the building and strode down the hall to the last door. Rapping sharply, he put his hand on the knob, but felt himself freeze. The old girl downstairs had said to just go on in, but before he could convince himself to do that, the door swung open and a tall, leggy redhead in a short khaki skirt and a tan silk blouse with the collar turned up stuck out her hand.

"Samuel Jayce, I assume."

For a moment, Sam couldn't quite find his tongue. This woman definitely did not put him in mind of his granny. What she put him in mind of was a million bucks, and with just that one look he felt like the lowliest plowboy in the county. Why hadn't he worn a suit? Maybe because he didn't own one. *Duh.* Sure enough, though, he should've worn something other than jeans. Well, it was too late for that now. Shaking himself, he belatedly clasped her hand. It felt long and smooth and delicate in his own much rougher one.

Only a few inches shorter than his own six feet, she had long, slender arms and legs and a neat little waist that called attention to the thrust of her high, firm breasts, while the graceful length of her neck led the eye upward to her face. Though a little square, the symmetry of her high cheekbones and the crisp line of her jaw, accentuated by the stubborn thrust of her chin, nevertheless struck Sam as amazingly feminine. She had a perfect nose, very delicately arched brows a couple shades darker than her bright, curly, upswept hair and big, round eyes of green hazel spoked with a soft blue. Her mouth was neither too full nor too thin, elegantly shaped and painted the same shiny pinkish-orange as her short, oval fingernails, like strawberries mixed with crushed coral. Her skin, a pale, flawless gold, literally shined with health and vigor.

By appearance alone, Sam would have put her at about his own age of twenty-four, but the cool perfection of her makeup and the graceful assurance with which she handled herself pegged her as older. Sharp interest, accompanied by an equally sharp sense of disappointment, momentarily blindsided him.

"Just call me Sam," he managed with what he feared was a frown and added too late, "ma'am."

Her mouth quirked at that, but she merely beckoned him into the office with a movement of her head. He let go of her hand, realizing suddenly that he'd held it too long, and tried not to gulp as he followed her through what looked like a sitting area furnished with castoffs which were probably in reality expensive antiques, not that he'd know a genuine collectible from fire kindling.

"You can leave your coat on the chair there," she said, turning in to an inner room. He shucked his coat, draped it over the back of a threadbare easy chair and walked into the other room. Pale wood file cabinets topped with an array of potted plants lined one rust-colored wall, and two tweedy, upholstered chairs stood before a sleek modern desk set at an angle to the front window. A bright floral carpet covered the floor and pale green curtains looped and draped about the windows. The executive leather chair behind the pale desk carried the cool green from the windows into the room.

Sierra Carlton performed a smooth little pirouette on the pointed toe of one high-heeled, tan leather shoe and walked behind the desk, dropping down into that high-backed chair. She couldn't have framed herself more perfectly. The contrast of that vibrant hair against the calm green was breathtaking.

"Won't you have a seat, Sam?"

"Thank you." He stepped in front of an armchair and sat, trying not to be dazzled by the bright, vibrant woman across the desk. Telling himself that it was time to take charge of this situation, he leaned forward slightly, elbows resting on the arms of the chair. "Ms. Carlton, I'm told—"

She lifted a slender hand, halting the flow of his words. "Sierra, please. Only seems fair if you're going to insist that I call you Sam."

Nodding, he got back to business. "I'm told, uh, *Sierra,* that you're planning to farm flowers on that hundred and sixty acres you bought northwest of town.''

She stiffened, pulling her shoulders back. His gaze fell instantly to the thrust of her breasts, and suddenly he had a problem of a different sort.

"What of it?" she demanded.

Jerking his gaze back up to her face, he willed himself to relax and lay out his cards. "Well, it's like this. You're wanting to do some farming, and I'm a farmer. Custom farming, it's called. See, usually I hire out to the landowner to perform any or all of the farming disciplines from field prep to harvest. I have a full line of equipment, ample experience and I've been reading up on flower crops. Once I get a good look at your property I'll be able to devise a planting program."

"A planting program," she echoed.

He spread his hands, warming to his subject. "Yeah, see, farming is organized, high-tech business now. We're still dependent on Mother Nature, but we don't leave any more to chance than we must. Now, most farming around here is being done on established fields, but that's ranch land you're sitting on out there, which isn't to say that it can't be farmed, because I believe it can, but it's going to take a lot of soil preparation and hard work."

She sat back, picked up an ink pen and began turning it end over end with her fingers. "I hope you'll pardon me for saying so, but you seem awful young for this."

"Yes, ma'am. Twenty-four last month, but I have a degree in agriculture from Texas A&M and plenty of personal references." He fished a folded sheet of paper from his shirt pocket and began unfolding it. "I've been in business for myself nearly four years, and I first hired out as a farmhand at fourteen, so I have nearly ten years experience."

She took the sheet of paper that he offered her and looked it over. "There are addresses here from Longview to El Paso. You've been around some."

"From the Piney Woods to the Rio Grande and the Red River to the Gulf of Mexico, but I've got to say as far as farming, this is the place to be. No other reason I'd come back here."

She blinked at that, and he realized with a sudden flush of heat that he'd said too much. Trying desperately to deflect her attention, he stumbled on.

"That and my baby sisters. Kim and Keli, they're seven. Twins. I understand you've got a little girl, too."

Sierra Carlton smiled and laid aside the sheet of references. "Yes. Tyree. She's eight, going on nine, as she'd be quick to remind me."

He nodded, praying he'd found ground common enough to allay any hint of doubt he might have inadvertently stirred. "Maybe they know each other, our girls."

"Could be. I'll ask Tyree."

He resisted the urge to swipe a hand over his face and instead tried to steer the subject back to business. "So, what do you think? Are you interested in taking me on? I'm convinced we could pull a profit at this if we go about it right."

She tapped the capped ink pen against her chin,

eyes narrowed in thought. "May I ask how you became aware of my intentions, Sam?"

He shifted uncomfortably. "Well, I heard about it down at the bank. Mr. Ontario's been real good to me. Gave me my first loan so I could buy equipment, helped me pay for it by referring me for work, and just recently we've established a line of credit for me so I can expand."

A bright smile lit her face. "Mr. Ontario told you about my plans? Frankly, I didn't think he approved."

That smile had the power to dazzle, and for a moment Sam was tempted to foster it, but one thing Sam believed in wholeheartedly was honesty, especially when it came to business dealings. He cleared his throat. "Um, well, to be honest, ma'am, he didn't exactly tell me what you were planning. I sort of, like, overheard him talking about it to someone else."

That amazing smile dimmed. "Oh?"

Sam shifted in his chair once more. "Yes, ma'am. I was sitting in his office when some fellow named Dinsmore called. I'm sure Mr. Ontario didn't mean to be indiscreet, but I couldn't help overhearing what was being said."

Disappointment stamped all over what remained of that smile. "I see."

For some reason he wanted to get up, go around that desk and hug her, or at least pat her on the shoulder. Instead, he sat forward and said with quiet conviction, "For what it's worth, ma'am, I disagree with Mr. Ontario on this. I mean, just because a thing hasn't been done in a certain area before doesn't mean that it can't be done or that it's foolish to try.''

She smiled again, but this time it was a warm, seemingly personal connection that did strange things inside his chest. ''What would you charge me for an undertaking such as this, from scratch, as you say?''

So there it was, the moment of reckoning. Sam eased forward in his seat and splayed his elbows on the edge of her desk, reaching forward to cup his hands together over the flowered border of her desk blotter. ''Well, there's the thing, ma'am. Sierra. This looks to be a very labor-intensive operation, and I'm guessing, frankly, that we're pretty evenly matched here. You've got the land, the funding and, I'm hoping, the market connections, while I've got the equipment, the know-how and the strong back. I'd say that makes for a pretty equal partnership.''

''Partnership?'' she repeated warily, and suddenly it was do or die.

''That's right,'' he said, forcing calmness into his voice though his insides were jumping like a bucket full of crickets. ''A clean fifty-fifty split. I don't see it working any other way.''

She blinked and huffed a long breath in and out. ''Hmm.'' She bit her lip, displaying the smooth, clean edges of her straight, white teeth, reminding him that the dentist had said the girls were going to need braces by middle school. Seconds ticked by. It was all he could do to sit back in his chair and wait without jiggling something. Finally she tossed down the pen and spread her hands.

"I hadn't thought of taking on a partner," she told him. "This isn't a decision I can make on the spur of the moment, you understand."

Defeat stabbed at him, but he fought it off with nonchalance. "Oh, sure, sure. I completely get that. You take a few days to think it over and let me know. Meanwhile, you might want to check out those references."

She pulled the paper toward her and glanced at it. "All right. I'll do that."

"You have my number," he said, sliding to the edge of his seat.

"Yes." She got to her feet and stuck out her hand. "Thank you for coming. This was...enlightening."

He took her hand in his and gave it a good shake. "Thank you for hearing me out, Sierra. I hope you'll decide soon because there's lots to do if we're going to have a crop this summer."

Smiling wanly, she placed both hands on her hips, glanced down at the desk and nodded. "You'll hear from me next week."

He had to be satisfied with that. She walked him out into the sitting room where he collected his coat, then all the way down the stairs to the front door of the shop. They chatted about the weather, bemoaning the gray skies and frigid winds with which they were beginning the new year and wondering if they would soon get precipitation and in what form. It was all very polite and formal. As soon as he stepped out onto that cold sidewalk, a feeling of doom descended on him, and he was suddenly very sure that he'd somehow blown it.

Well, he'd give it a week, anyway. He could afford to do that and still have plenty of time to make other arrangements if she didn't go for the deal. It wouldn't be the first time he'd been refused, but something about this meeting rankled deep within him. He couldn't have said why, but as he walked along the street to the battered double-cab, dually pickup parked in a lot behind the city hall, Sam felt his stomach churn with failure.

Sierra slid along the shop window, watching Sam Jayce stride down the street with a long-stepping, shoulder-rocking swagger, his hands tucked into the pockets of his coat. She didn't really know what she'd expected to find in Sam Jayce, but she sure hadn't expected such a supremely confident and accomplished *young* man.

Moments after Sam left the building, Bette came into the showroom in answer to the door chime in case they had a customer. Sierra didn't turn around as she asked, "So, what do you think?"

"I think I wish I was at least fifteen years younger and fifty pounds lighter."

Sierra glanced around with a wry smile. "He is pretty cute."

"Cute!" Bette snorted. "Honey, you've been alone too long if those shoulders and that butt don't strike you a little harder than *cute*."

"He's just a kid," Sierra said dismissively. And he just might be the answer to her prayers.

A partnership, though. Pride rebelled at the notion. She was determined to make a success of herself, no matter what her father or anyone else thought, but Frank McAfree already believed that his daughter was completely incapable of handling her own finances, let alone her life. She could just imagine what he would say if she took on a partner, especially such a young, *attractive* partner, because no one could deny that Sam Jayce, whatever his age, was a very attractive man.

He'd put her in mind of a robust young Julius Caesar, even with that spiked, sandy brown hair. It was the shape of his head, from the perfect oval of his skull to his high forehead and prominent nose down to the square, blunt strength of his chin, which gave him that calmly powerful air. He had dimples that gouged into the lean planes of his cheeks, sleepy, pale green eyes thickly fringed with gold-tipped lashes and a perfectly sculpted mouth that added an almost feminine counterweight to the harshly masculine proportions of his face. But the rest of that package contained nothing even remotely feminine.

He wasn't a huge man, maybe six feet tall and long and lean with broad shoulders and compact muscles that bunched and elongated with fluid power as he moved. She couldn't help noticing the size and strength of his hands, the way his well-rounded thighs filled out his jeans, and yes, the rear view was enough to make a woman look twice. She just wished he was about ten or twenty years older.

On the other hand, perhaps his youth was in his favor. All the older men to whom she had proposed farming flowers had treated her like a foolish child. Maybe Sam Jayce was just young enough to still believe in dreams and brash enough to try to make them come true. But how could she know?

She would check his references, of course, but any name listed there would have been chosen because it guaranteed a glowing report. Better to speak with someone with no vested interest, someone in a position to know the scuttlebutt. It was time to pay a visit to an old friend.

The January wind cut like a knife when she got out of the sleek foreign luxury car that had been her first real indulgence after receiving her unexpected inheritance from dear old Edwin Searle. To say that finding herself among Edwin's heirs had been a shock was a serious understatement, but the kind of money that he had left her, Avis and Valerie was the stuff of which dreams were made. It was also an awesome responsibility, and one with which Sierra was having a difficult time coping, though she wouldn't have admitted it even to her own shadow.

The wind tugged at her jacket as she sprinted across the parking lot toward the coffee shop in the strip mall where she had originally opened her floral business. If anyone could tell her about Sam Jayce, it would be the coffee-shop proprietor Gwyn Dunstan. Sierra shoved through the heavy glass door and came to a halt just inside as the welcome fragrance of hot coffee and fresh-baked goods warmed her.

"Hey!" Gwyn greeted her cheerily, moving across the floor with steaming mugs and plates of oozing cinnamon rolls balanced in her hands.

The place was fairly busy, the cold Texas wind having driven folks indoors for a hot, fragrant cup and warm roll. Nevertheless, Gwyn quickly deposited the cups and saucers at a table of four men and called her teenage daughter from the back. "Molly!" Gwyn came toward Sierra with her arms open wide. "Looking good there, girlfriend. How's life treating you?"

"Good. How about you?" Sierra returned the hug. Though known for her cynicism and caustic tongue, Gwyn was a warmer creature than many suspected, and lately she seemed softer, cheerier. She still retained that core of inner toughness that made her Gwyn, however.

"Same old, same old," Gwyn said lightly as Molly appeared from the kitchen.

"Hi, Sierra." Blond, pretty Molly had her mom's same thin, taut, muscular build but with a nubile softness that drew boys like flies to honey. She occasionally baby-sat Sierra's daughter. "How's Tyree?"

"Looking forward to her birthday, which isn't until the very last day of March. And we just passed New Year's, for pity's sake."

"Kids," Gwyn said. "They live from holiday to holiday."

"Well, let us know when you put her party together," Molly said.

"Absolutely," Sierra promised, then she turned to Gwyn. "Can we talk?"

"Sure thing. Let's snag a cup and head back into the office."

Two minutes later, they were seated around the small metal table that Gwyn used as a desk in the cubbyhole behind the kitchen. "So what's up? Dennis still giving you a hard time?"

"Perpetually, but I'm not here to talk about the magic reappearing ex."

Dennis had turned up after a three-year absence—just as soon as the news of her inheritance had reached him—and he'd made her life miserable ever since. His influence had turned her formerly sweet, loving eight-year-old into a greedy demanding brat that Sierra sometimes didn't even recognize.

"What do you know about a young man named Sam Jayce?"

Gwyn's eyebrows went straight up. "Why do you ask?"

"I'm thinking about going into business with him."

Gwyn sat back and folded her arms. "You remember that woman who was murdered a few years back?"

Sarah Jayce. No wonder Sam's name had

sounded familiar. "She was that woman beaten to death by her husband."

Gwyn nodded. "She was also Sam's mother."

"Ohmigod."

"Jonah Jayce was a brutal drunk. He beat her to death because she hid their baby girls from him."

"Twins," Sierra remembered.

"That's right. Sarah was afraid, apparently with good reason, that Jonah would hurt them. Sam himself was long gone by the time they were born. He left home at fourteen, went to foster care at his mother's insistence. A neighbor boy to the west of me was best friends with Sam. I remember that Sam's foster mother used to drop him off so the boys could spend time together. He was always very polite, Sam was."

"He still is," Sierra murmured.

"Not surprised." Gwyn shifted forward in her chair. "I heard that Jonah used to get drunk and show up at his foster home spoiling for a fight, and that's why Sam dropped out of high school at sixteen and disappeared. He was twenty when his mom died. They must've been in contact because he showed up, assumed guardianship of his baby sisters and disappeared again. A year later the three of them moved back into the Jayce house about six miles west of town, and somehow that boy convinced old Zeke Ontario down at the bank to take a chance on him and started buying up equipment. Calls himself a 'custom farmer.' I hear he's got a college education and a keen business sense. You could do worse."

Sierra sat back with an expelled breath. "Wow. Gwyn, if your customers ever knew you retained this much about them... Sounds like life gave Sam lemons and he got busy making lemonade."

Gwyn nodded. "I'll tell you something else. He's utterly devoted to those two little girls. I don't think he has any sort of social life apart from them, and they're happy, well-adjusted children, which is surprising, given everything they've been through. I know that for a fact because Molly baby-sat them for a couple weeks last summer. She had a killer crush on Sam for a while after."

"I can imagine," Sierra muttered, and Gwyn laughed.

"Yeah, he's the sort to make the girls' hearts go flitter-flutter, all right, not that he seems to notice."

Sierra smiled, deliberately ignoring that, and picked up her coffee cup. "Thanks, Gwyn. I knew I could get the straight dope from you. Now tell me how you've been doing."

Gwyn chatted about the recent improvement in her business and her concerns about Avis, who had been keeping mostly to herself. Genuinely interested, Sierra listened and nodded, sipping her excellent coffee. But in the back of her mind, she felt a little "flitter-flutter" of her own. Not because of Sam's masculine, clean-cut good looks, of course—she wasn't a teenager—but rather with the possibility that she might have found the means to making her dreams come true.

At least that's what she told herself.

Chapter Two

Sierra glanced at the clock on the wall for the tenth time in as many minutes. She felt ridiculously nervous, and telling herself that she had nothing to *be* nervous about didn't help. Her doubts about Sam Jayce as a business partner had been completely put to rest by her attorney, Corbett Johnson, who had confirmed everything that Gwyn had told Sierra about Sam Jayce and then some.

Not only had Sam put himself through college, taken on the responsibility of rearing his little sisters and convinced the notoriously conservative local banker to back him in business, he'd paid off the mortgage on the small house and forty acres that he and his sisters had inherited from their mother. In Corbett's opinion, it was only a matter of time before Sam turned up a blinding success, fulfilling the expectations of apparently everyone who'd dealt with him. At the attorney's urging, Sierra had let him draw up the partnership papers, which she intended to present to Sam today as a *fait accompli* subtly designed to assure her the upper hand. She doubted he'd go for it, but the papers left room for compromise, while still guaranteeing her the majority of control.

By the time Sam arrived—precisely on time and looking even more breathtaking than before in dark, heavily starched jeans, a simple white T-shirt and a fitted black corduroy jacket—Sierra's heart was flittering and fluttering again. Maintaining a cool facade, she neatened the lay of her sophisticated surplice blouse, greeted him through the door she'd left standing open and waved him on into her office. His gaze flickered over her, and she felt her pulse quicken.

"Thank you for coming, Sam. Please be seated." Sierra noticed a large gold college ring on his right hand.

He tugged at the sides of his coat and sat. "I guess you've thought it over."

"Yes, I have, and I've decided to accept your offer."

The smile that elicited crinkled his eyes at the corners, cut deep grooves into his dimpled cheeks and flashed an impressive expanse of strong, white teeth. Suddenly her heart wasn't just flitter-fluttering; it was beating madly inside her chest like a wild thing trying to break free. Alarmed by her own reaction, Sierra forced herself to get down to business, sounding brusquer than she'd intended.

"I took the liberty of having papers drawn up, so if you'll just sign, we can get on with planning our new venture." As she spoke, she pushed two sets of stapled papers toward him, placed an ink pen on the desk between them and sat back, aware of his deepening frown.

He began thumbing through one set of papers. "You had papers drawn up? No discussion? No negotiation?"

Her confident smile faltered. "What's to discuss? You spelled out the particulars yourself, fifty-fifty on the profits. You provide expertise, equipment and labor. I provide land and financing."

He looked up, nailing her with a direct look launched from beneath the jut of his brows. "Says here that you get final approval on all expenditures."

"I am providing the funds."

"What about unexpected expenses—fuel, tools, research material, mechanical failures? They happen, you know, even with new machinery."

She shrugged. "We'll work out some sort of system."

"Over which you get final approval."

"Someone has to."

He got to his feet. "Right, and since you're the older one, that's naturally you." He shook his head bitterly. "No matter how hard I work, how much I know, how many times I'm proven right, I can't change the date of my birth." He pointed a finger at her, adding, "And don't you dare tell me time will take care of it."

He was right, of course, but this was business, and she would be foolish in the extreme not to try to take the upper hand. Wouldn't she? "Sam, I didn't mean to offend you. I'm just trying to protect my investment."

"Well, that goes for both of us," he said, swiping one set of papers off the desk and rolling them into a tube in his hands. "I'll just let *my* attorney look these over and get back to you."

"Yes, of course," she said softly, feeling slightly ashamed and uncertain.

He turned and walked out without another word, the rigid lines of his back making his anger obvious.

Evidently she had miscalculated. She'd assumed that his youth would naturally compel him to follow her lead. Instead, she'd let him know that she considered his age a tool to use against him. Brilliant.

Sierra dropped her head into her hands. She had just insulted her best hope of proving herself as a businesswoman. So much for her future as a flower producer. Biting her lip, she considered running after him, but in the end she didn't bother. If she let him walk out, chances were he'd just phone in his refusal and that would be that. On the other hand, if she ran after him, he'd demand more than she could give. Either way, the partnership seemed doomed. And, as usual, she had no one to thank but herself.

* * *

Sam yanked open the shop door and stepped out onto the sidewalk, executing a sharp right turn. As he stalked down the street he slapped the rolled papers against his thigh. So she was gorgeous, stylish, self-assured, wealthy and older than him—did that give her any right to treat him like a stupid, wet-behind-the-ears *kid?* He'd been beating himself up for days because he was sure he'd blown the best opportunity ever to come his way, and all along she'd just been waiting to cut him down to size.

Well, it was probably for the best. Hooking up in any way with Sierra Carlton would undoubtedly be a very bad mistake; an uneven partnership always was. Besides, she was too good-looking for comfort. The last thing he needed was a business partner who could distract him just with the blouse she chose to wear.

Hadn't she realized that little wrap thing wasn't conducive to a business meeting? Or was that the point? He could've stripped her with just the pull of that string tied at her waist. Didn't she realize that? Maybe she'd intended to distract him, or maybe she wasn't as smart as she looked. Just because she was older didn't mean she knew everything. If she did, she'd know that anything personal between them was never going to happen. Not in *his* business. Who needed her anyway?

Unfortunately, he did.

The sad truth was that Sierra Carlton and her flower farm were still the best opportunity that he had found to get out from under his equipment payment and make some sort of stable future for himself and the girls.

Mouth thinning into a compressed line, Sam slowed his asphalt-eating strides and blew out an agitated breath. Dismay rose up and threatened to choke him, but his pride still stung so sharply that for a moment he couldn't let himself feel the other. Then, gradually, the cold air began to clear his head.

Surely there was room for compromise. She had to know that he'd expect some leeway. She wasn't an airhead, despite evidence to the contrary from that slinky, formfitting, crisscrossed little top.

He briefly squeezed his eyes shut. Why couldn't she have just approached him as an equal? They could've hammered out an agreement in no time. It probably wouldn't have looked a lot different than the one in his hand, but at least it would have been a mutually made agreement. He'd handled negotiations before, after all. He knew how they worked. Mentally reviewing past negotiations, he tried to enumerate the ways in which Sierra had screwed up this one and, therefore, deserved his scorn.

By the time he reached his heavy-duty truck, he'd worked his way around to a distasteful but honest conclusion. If a man had presented him with that contract he wouldn't have been nearly as offended. Men always tried to one-up each other in a negotiation. It was expected. Moreover, if it had been grandmotherly Bette Grouper who had presented him with such a proposal, he probably would have signed without a quibble as a matter of re-

spect. But it had been Sierra Carlton who'd drawn
up that contract without input from him. Sexy, delicious Sierra Carlton.

He didn't like where that conclusion inevitably
led him. He wasn't upset because Sierra hadn't
shown the proper and expected respect for him as
a business partner, but because she'd treated him
"man to man," not as a man, and an attractive one
to boot.

Disgusted with himself, he unlocked the door and
got into the truck. Unrolling the paper against the
steering wheel, he carefully read every word. It
wasn't a bad deal, all told, with one or two excep-
tions that could be easily fixed. It shouldn't take
more than a couple of days to have his attorney
look this over and offer a few suggestions. It would
mean swallowing his pride, but he'd choked down
worse. That's what a real man would do, and nobody—but nobody—would ever be able to say that
Samuel Ray Jayce wasn't the real deal. Meanwhile,
he'd make sure that he got his business sense out
of his pants.

Sierra looked up from her desk a couple days
later to find Sam Jayce hanging his elbows in her
doorway. The sides of his cattleman's coat were
pulled wide, highlighting the powerful depth of his
chest and the slimness of his hips. The cold, breezy
weather had reddened his face and brought a sharp
clarity to those unusual sage-green eyes. For a moment he said nothing, merely stood there, hipshot,
regarding her implacably. Then abruptly he dropped

his arms and strolled toward her desk, one hand reaching around behind him.

Time slowed to a crawl, affording her fanciful mind space to conjure impossible scenarios. He would walk to her desk, skirting it to reach her side, reach down, pull her up out of her chair and slam his mouth down over hers. No. He would skirt her desk, circle behind her chair, tilt it backward with his big hands and slowly lean in for a melting kiss. Or perhaps it would be a combination of the two. He would pull her to her feet, cup her face in his hands and deliver that melting kiss erect.

Her heart was pounding by the time he slapped a folded packet of papers onto her desk. She jumped, and the spell was broken. Color flamed in her cheeks.

"S-Sam."

"Page three," he said, pointing at the papers.

With trembling fingers, she unfolded the papers and peeled back the top two. An addendum had been typewritten in the space between the paragraphs indicating that a special account for expenses would be set up, the sum of which would be determined by an accountant furnished with estimates by Sam himself. Sierra could name the accountant. Scrupulously fair. Relief swam through Sierra as she reached for a pen and scribbled her initials in the space provided.

"Is this it?"

"Page four."

She lifted the page and scanned the words. He had added four hundred dollars a month to the modest salary she had proposed, the sum of which would be taken from his year-end profits. She had expected him to double it but realized that she couldn't very well make that proposal herself. He'd think she was patronizing him. She would have to make certain that the expense budget was generous.

She inscribed her initials again and, without comment, flipped over to the final page to sign her name in the space provided. He produced a second set of papers, and she memorialized those while he made good on the first set. When the second set was fully formalized, he folded the first and slid them into a coat pocket before sinking down onto the corner of her desk.

"Okay. Now that that's out of the way, I need some idea from you about what you're hoping to plant."

She leaned back in her chair and tried not to look at those hard thighs on her desk. Inches from her hand. "Annuals tend to provide the showiest single-stem blossoms for flower arranging, but there are a number of perennials useful in arrangements, as well. I've put together a list of about a dozen plants." She opened a drawer and extracted the paper she'd been working on. "I hope you can read my writing."

He glanced at the sheet, nodded and said, "I'll manage." Folding the paper, he stowed it with the partnership agreement. "I'll need to do some more research and get back to you."

"When would you like to meet next?"

"Saturday work for you?"

"I don't usually work on Saturdays, but the shop is open, so it's no problem."

He shook his head. "Not here. Out at the farm. I need to get a close look at the fields."

"Of course. All right. Just come on up to the house whenever you like."

"It'll be early," Sam warned. "There's lots to do."

"Really? At this time of year? I thought the real work wouldn't begin until early spring."

He stood. "You thought wrong. It'll take pretty much every daylight minute between now and planting time to get the planning done and those fields ready."

Surprised, Sierra nodded. "I see. Um, how early?"

"Daylight," Sam said cheerily. She didn't quite manage to keep the dismay off her face, and he chuckled. "Okay, eight."

"Not much better," she muttered.

He moved toward the door, tossing a wry smile over his shoulder on the way. "You're the one who wanted to be a farmer. Of course, daylight comes a lot earlier in spring and summer, which is when the real work is done."

Completely willing to humiliate herself in order to foster the easygoing banter, she made an exaggerated face of distaste.

Laughing, Sam reached into his coat pocket, extracted the agreement and saluted her with it. "See you Saturday. Partner."

Partner. It sounded even better than she'd imagined.

*   *   *

Sam gazed around the high-ceilinged, octagonal foyer without expression. Sierra watched him take in the little artistic setbacks displaying vases of fresh flowers, naturally, and the open, sweeping staircase before he looked pointedly at the mug in her hands.

"Coffee smells good."

Sierra tried not to show her surprise, though why she should be surprised by the fact that Sam enjoyed a cup of coffee early of a morning she didn't know. Coffee was "in" with the younger generation these days. Funny, the longer she knew him, the older Sam seemed.

"Come on in, and I'll get you a cup," she said, turning down the central hall.

Glancing over her shoulder, she caught him looking from room to room as they passed, but her smile of pride died when she saw the frown he was wearing. So, he didn't approve of her house, either. For Pete's sake, it wasn't as if she'd built a replica of the Taj Mahal. A quarter-million dollars happened to buy a lot in their corner of Texas, but not *that* much. The house was only 3,500 square feet, with three bedrooms and a study upstairs, where Tyree and Bette's teenage daughter, Chelsea, now slept, and the living areas all downstairs.

The house looked elegant and expensive, much like the house in which she'd grown up, but with contrast-colored picture-framing on the walls and lots of arches and display niches and plenty of ceramic tile and lush carpeting on the floors. She'd put her money into the infrastructure, believing that it was best to build to last, and cut some corners on the fixtures, going for unique rather than expensive, but still she'd caught major flak from her father and bankers for spending too much.

She led Sam into the bright, white-tile-and-natural-woods kitchen with its cheery yellow-and-orange accents, took a cup from the cabinet and filled it with the best freshly brewed coffee that money could buy. "Take anything in it?"

"No, thanks." He gestured toward the breakfast nook, pulling papers from his coat pocket. "Why don't we sit and take a look at what I've come up with?"

"Sure."

While he shrugged out of his coat and hung it on the back of a chair at the table, she placed his mug in front of him and sat down on his right. He sat, unfolded the papers and reached for his cup.

"Mmm, excellent. Now these are planting guides for the dozen blooms you stipulated and about ten more that lend themselves easily to our climate." He shifted a specific paper toward her and added, "These are the bestselling exotics, but we'll get into those later."

"How many acres do you propose we plant?"

"I'll know better when I get a look at the fields, but I suspect we'll only want to put about a third of our—that is, your—acreage into cultivation."

Sierra frowned. She'd envisioned the whole 160 acres ablaze in summer blooms. "Why is that?"

"It's just good land management. Flowers and vegetables take lots of soil preparation. They require lots of nutrients. By rotating our fields, we can protect the viability of the soil and the quality of our crops. We'll plant some cover crops and plow those under in order to feed the soil, but a third of the fields will simply lie fallow year to year. Fortunately, flowers are a high-yield, high-return product, so our acreage is more than sufficient. In fact, it's quite abundant."

"You've really done your research," she observed.

He nodded, drank from his cup and went on. "We'll need help initially. Flower farming, like vegetable farming, is a labor-intensive operation. Bear that in mind when you look over the cost estimates. Overall, the amount of soil preparation needed this first year will dictate how much initial profit we make, but I think a conservative estimate is twenty to twenty-five thousand."

Sierra tried not to gasp in dismay. "That's all?"

"Per acre."

"Oh." What she really meant was *"Wow!"*

"That'll rise after we get over the hump of initial investment and figure out exactly what our soil will best support," he went on. "The worst areas should probably go into lavender. It's hardy, practically grows itself and is useful for sachets, perfumes, dried flowers and filler. Sunflowers are another hardy pick with multiple uses. The showier blooms are the more profitable, of course, so our best fields will go to those. We'll be planting strips of rye and wheat around the perimeters of those fields to protect the blooms from the wind and get those nice, straight stems that you floral designers are so crazy about."

"I never even thought of that," she admitted.

He just shrugged and went on, his enthusiasm positively infectious. "We may have to do some irrigating, but I actually own a few sections of aboveground irrigation equipment that I took in trade for some work I did last year, and we have our own well here, so that's not a major concern."

Sierra sat back and regarded him frankly. "I have to say, I'm impressed."

"Good," he said. "That means you'll listen while I make this next proposal."

She would've listened to him read the weather report, but then realized that was very likely to happen, considering the business they were now in. "Let's hear it."

"Greenhouses. They'll add to the initial outlay, but not as much as you may think. We'll need two for start. One we'll use to germinate seedlings. The other will allow us to grow the more exotic blooms that our general climate prohibits. I can design and build them myself. They're very simple structures, actually, but I won't lie to you. They could be expensive to operate. We'll have to keep the lights on sixteen hours a day, control the climate 24/7 and do lots of watering. But the returns can be very substantial."

Sierra bit her lip, excited but leery. One thing she'd learned the hard way was that money spent fast. "Let's take a look at the cost estimates."

They put their heads together over the numbers, and Sierra found herself dismayed. "Sam, that's nearly all of my capital."

"Surely you weren't thinking of pouring cash into this," he said.

"Why take out loans when you have cash?" she demanded.

"Because it's smarter," he explained. "Look. If you take out a loan and the proposition fails, you're going to lose some property and some money, but you'll also have money left. Once money's spent, though, it's gone. Yours should be tied up in long-term investment."

"Most of it is."

"It should stay that way."

"But you pay interest on borrowed money."

"And you *make* interest on invested money, which you use as a kind of collateral to secure your loans."

"Tell that to the bankers," Sierra retorted. "They won't loan me money."

"Well, that doesn't make any sense."

She glanced around her uneasily and admitted, "It's this house."

He hooked an elbow over the back of his chair and looked around. "It's quite a house, but I don't see the problem unless you owe more against it than it's worth."

"That's the thing," she said warily. "I don't owe

anything against this house, and I absolutely refuse to use it as collateral.''

He stared at her for a moment. ''You actually paid cash for this house?''

She lifted her chin defiantly. ''Yes. A quarter of a million dollars. And I'd do it again.''

He just shook his head. ''Women!''

''I beg your pardon.''

''Don't get your shorts in a twist, er, panties.'' He waved that away, too. ''What I mean is that women seem to have a peculiar anxiety about the security of their homes. My mom was the same way.''

At the mention of his mother, his voice became wistful. It completely destroyed whatever resentment his earlier exclamation had dealt Sierra.

''What happened to your mother was a truly awful thing, Sam.''

His light green eyes met hers. ''She stayed married to him because she was afraid to be without a home and, I guess, because he convinced her that she deserved what he dished out.'' He looked away, and a muscle flexed in the hollow of his jaw. ''Nothing I could say or do seemed to make any difference.''

She reached out instinctively and curled her fingers around his. ''I'm so sorry, Sam. That's such a tough thing you and your sisters have had to go through.''

He gripped her hand and smiled thinly. ''The only good thing my father ever did in his whole miserable life was give us those girls.'' His grin broadened, and the light of genuine affection and pride lit his eyes with a warmth she hadn't seen before. "Seeing them happy, it makes up for so much."

Sierra thought of Tyree and said, "I know what you mean." The problem was that Tyree didn't seem happy anymore.

"I see so much of Mom in them," Sam was saying, "and no matter how screwed up her head was about Jonah, she protected them with her very life."

"Oh, Sam," Sierra heard herself saying even as she watched her hand rise and settle gently against the curve of his jaw. Their eyes met again. And held. Awareness flared in those fascinating green eyes, like miniature sunbursts, and Sierra realized with jolting certainty that this was no *boy* sitting here next to her. This was a man, very much a man, and a rare one at that.

As amazing at it seemed, she may have picked the right man at the right time. For once.

Chapter Three

Sam sat back, aware that he'd nearly made a very bad mistake. He'd actually thought about kissing her. Even in the best of circumstances, Sierra Carlton was not the sort of woman with whom he could afford to fool around. She was his business partner. Business and romance never mixed well. The repercussions could be fatal, at least to the enterprise. Only a fool would jeopardize a financial setup this good, even if she hadn't been so smart with her money in the past.

Quickly retreating to the safety of business, Sam said, "We're burning daylight here. I'd better get out and take a good look at those fields."

Sierra set down her coffee cup as she rose from

her chair. "Finish your coffee while I grab my coat, and we'll take off."

He gulped. "You don't have to go."

"Oh, I want to. I've been looking forward to it."

He tried not to sound panicked when he asked, "What about your daughter?"

"She's taken care of. I had Chelsea Grouper stay over last night."

Sam smiled weakly as she spun out of the room, then hunkered down over his cup. What was wrong with him? He knew how a man had to behave in a business situation. The fact that his partner was a woman shouldn't make any difference.

Maybe he should start paying some attention to his social life. It had been a long time since he'd been with a woman. Shoot, he'd never been with a woman. He'd been with his share of grown-up girls, but not in some time, and he'd never been with a real woman, at least not one the caliber of Sierra Carlton. Somehow, she had a way of making him supremely aware of that fact. He rubbed his brow and chugged back the remaining brew in his cup.

Sierra reappeared wearing a bright yellow down jacket over her long-sleeved knit top and jeans. She was a woman who looked as good in jeans and boots and a fat, bushy ponytail as designer suits and more elaborate hairstyles. He wondered if she permed her hair and suppressed the urge to wrap a corkscrew curl at the nape of her neck around his finger as he followed her to the back door. They stepped down into a three-car garage that was empty except for her expensive sedan.

"We should take my truck," he pointed out belatedly.

"Oh. Right. Should've thought of that. This way, then." She led him through a side door and around the house to the front, where he'd parked his truck at the top of the graveled, circular drive.

He hadn't bothered to lock up, and she was inside before he even had the chance to go for her door, which irked him mildly, though he told himself that equals didn't bother opening doors for one another, even if one of them was female.

"Where's the gate?" he asked, settling behind the wheel.

"Gate? The property's only fenced on two sides. Is that a problem?"

"Naw, not really. Barbed wire will only keep the big critters out, anyway. We may want to string some chicken wire, though."

"I'm beginning to realize how much I don't know," she muttered, reaching for her safety belt.

"That's what I'm here for."

He slid the key into the ignition and started the truck, but before he could put the transmission into gear, she reached across and clapped a hand over his forearm.

"Put on your seat belt first."

The admonition flew through him. Before he could think, certainly before he could reason, he had shaken off her hand and snapped, "You may be my partner, but you aren't my mother!"

Her mouth dropped open, and matching ire

flashed in her blue-green eyes. "I'm not trying to be!"

"Aren't you?"

"No! You're in the car, you put a belt on."

"You have to get over this age thing, Sierra, or we just can't work together."

"What has this got to do with age?" She threw up her hands. "You've spent the morning proving how invaluable you are. Is it so surprising that I don't want you taking unnecessary chances with your personal safety?"

"We aren't going to drive on the interstate."

"If your sisters were in this truck, wouldn't you expect them to buckle up?"

That set him back. If the girls had been in the truck, he'd have buckled his seat belt without even thinking about it, because he always did when they were with him and because he always insisted that they do the same. Maybe he'd gotten in the habit of not fastening the thing when he was working on the farm, but that was no excuse. He tamped down his unreasonable anger and felt embarrassment rise in its place. He closed his eyes, set his jaw, then made himself relax it again.

"You're right." He pulled the seat belt across him and shoved the hasp into the clip next to his hip, then he yanked the transmission into gear and set off down a track alongside the house, probably worn down during construction.

"You're the one who has a problem with your age," she grumbled.

"Well, if I do," he retorted, "it's because so

many other people have shown me that it's a problem for them.''

"I understand that," she told him, "but I'm not one of them. So far you've demonstrated great maturity—despite that little outburst just now."

He pointed a look at her. "And you didn't have a little outburst just now?"

She looked away, one hand going to a curl that had worked its way free in front of her ear. "Well, yeah, I did." She turned an impish smile on him. "But nobody's ever accused me of demonstrating maturity."

He laughed, resentment waning. "I like honesty in a woman."

She cut her eyes at him. "I'll try always to be honest with you, Sam."

Desire slugged him straight in the groin. He jerked his gaze forward, then hunched over the wheel, silently cursing the restrictions of that belt. "Th-that's good. Partners should be honest with one another."

"We're going to be good together. I know we are."

He nearly burst his zipper. Abruptly, he guided the truck off the trail to the left, hoping that the buck and bounce of crossing rough ground would prove an adequate distraction for both of them.

Sierra pushed back into her seat. "What are you doing?"

"Just trying to get the lay of the land."

So much for honesty.

* * *

"I'm not sure I should've let you talk me into this," Sierra murmured, stepping up into the bank lobby with Sam at her side.

"The door swings both ways," he reminded her succinctly. "I don't know what you're carping about, though. It's my credit."

"But I'm supposed to provide the capital."

"You are. You're securing my credit with your capital and reestablishing your own in the process. Without risking your precious home, I might add."

Sierra sighed, convinced again but still not liking it. He was taking a huge chance by putting his own credit rating on the line like this. For her dream. She wasn't entirely persuaded that it was going to work out, though. Surely no one would loan such a young man the kind of money they were seeking.

Zeke Ontario came out of his office and strode toward them, hand outstretched. "Sam. Sierra. I'm surprised to see you two here together."

Sam spoke up before Sierra had a chance to do so. "Sierra and I have entered into a partnership, Zeke."

"Not that flower thing," the banker said impatiently.

"That very promising flower thing," Sam confirmed, nodding at Sierra, "and we've got the figures to prove it."

Sierra held out the large envelope that contained their papers and lifted her chin. "What would you say to an initial profit of twenty-five thousand per acre?"

Zeke Ontario's bushy gray eyebrows went straight up, but to Sierra's irritation, he looked to Sam for confirmation. "Is this true?"

"You know I like to err on the conservative side, Zeke," Sam drawled.

"Well," the elderly banker said, sweeping an arm toward his office, "let's have us a little chat then."

"Thought you'd say that," Sam teased, laying his hand in the small of Sierra's back and ushering her forward.

Sierra felt a little thrill of victory. Or was it something else?

She tried to push that aside as she preceded the men into the office. To her deep personal embarrassment, she was beginning to feel too much attraction to her young partner, and she could just imagine what her father would say to that if he should ever learn of it. He still hadn't forgiven her for eloping with Dennis Carlton ten years ago, and it didn't help that he'd been right about Dennis, either.

She'd been a foolish nineteen-year-old, at odds with her father since the death of her mother some seven years earlier. She'd been so sure that Dennis would give her the affection and approval that her father hadn't, but she'd been nothing more to Dennis than his ticket to the easy life. By the time Dennis realized that marrying the boss's daughter had actually achieved the opposite of what he'd hoped, Sierra had been pregnant with Tyree. When it had become apparent that not even the birth of his granddaughter would soften Frank's intractable disapproval, Dennis had split for greener pastures and only kept in contact with Tyree intermittently until news of Sierra's inheritance had reached him. Now both her father and her ex were tugging at her again. Her father was trying to dictate her life while Dennis was doing his best to squeeze money out of her via their daughter.

Sam seated her in front of Mr. Ontario's desk and dropped down into the chair next to her while Zeke made his lumbering way to his own place. Sierra removed papers from the portfolio, placed them on the desk and explained each one. The banker studied the papers, listened attentively, then looked to Sam. Again.

"Did you put this together, Sam?"

"Yes. They're solid figures, Zeke. I've cited my sources carefully."

"Of course. Hmm." He studied the papers a few minutes longer, then hit the intercom on his desk and asked for a loan officer to be sent in before kicking back in his chair. "I had no idea flowers could be so profitable. You've put together a good business plan. We'll check your sources, and if they pan out, which I'm sure they will, I don't see any problem, especially with Sierra's backing."

Sierra stiffened, but she'd barely gotten her mouth open before Sam said firmly, "Sierra's not 'backing me,' Zeke. I told you already. We're part-ners. This whole thing was Sierra's idea, as you well know."

The old banker had the good grace to look cha-grined. He actually tried to smile at Sierra. She

looked down her nose at the old chauvinist, then
flashed Sam a grateful smile. He winked, patiently
awaiting the loan officer.

Sam was feeling pretty good when they walked
out of the bank. The sun was shining, the ambient
temperature had risen to almost forty degrees, and
the first installment of a considerable sum of money
had been deposited into his and Sierra's joint business account—S & S Farms. They'd pulled the
name out of thin air on the spur of the moment,
joking about whose initial should come first. Zeke
had suggested that they look into incorporation, and
they'd agreed to discuss the idea with her attorney,
Corbett Johnson. This thing was coming together.
He had a good feeling about it, and from the way
Sierra was smiling at him, he'd say she did, too.

"Thank you."

"For what?" he asked, surprised.

"Zeke Ontario would never have given me that
loan."

Sam shrugged negligently. The truth was that he
hadn't much liked the dismissive manner in which
the man had treated Sierra. So she hadn't done the
smartest thing when it came to her house; she
could've done worse. Besides, he figured it was un-
derstandable. A single mother with a child to raise
would do almost anything to secure her home.
Maybe she need not have spent so much, but the
shock of all that money must've gone to her head.
Heck, he'd spent that much and more on farming
equipment.

"Zeke's a good guy, but he's pretty old school," Sam told her.

"Meaning that he thinks women make good tellers and not much more."

Sam chuckled. "True, but he gave me a break when I needed it most, and I have to be grateful for that."

"Yes, of course you do. And so do I since you're my partner now."

He rubbed his hands together eagerly. "Can't wait to get started, frankly."

"When do you intend to start breaking ground or whatever it is you do first?"

Sam looked up at the bright winter sky, then down at the even brighter woman strolling along at his side. "Now seems like a pretty good time."

Sierra stopped in her tracks. "You mean this very minute."

He squinted at the sun overhead. "I think I can get a load of fertilizer and most of the equipment out to the farm by dark." Impulsively, he tapped her on the end of her nose. "By the time you get home tomorrow evening, I might even have that little bottom patch tilled."

"It'll be a real farm then."

"So it will."

She laughed and shook her head, and for one heart-stopping moment he thought she might actually throw her arms around him, but then she just clapped them on her sides and laughed some more. He laughed, too, as he walked her the rest of the way to her storefront, and somehow the sun seemed to shine even brighter, as bright as the future. Their future.

Frank McAfree dumped his coat on the living room sofa and brought his hands to his hips in what Sierra thought of as his classical ''rant'' pose.

''What the devil is going on?''

''Well, hello, Dad, nice to see you, too. Glad you could drop by.''

''Don't change the subject, Sierra. I asked you a question.''

Sierra folded her arms protectively. His carrot-red hair had turned yellow-white in the last few years, and his square face was sagging a bit at the jawline, but he'd lost none of his imposing authority. He'd always seemed larger than life.

''I assume you are referring to the plowing and the greenhouse.''

''Please tell me you haven't sunk your funds into some harebrained scheme.''

''As a matter of fact, I haven't.''

''Then why plow up all that ground? And just how big of a greenhouse do you need, anyway?''

''My partner and I have decided—''

''Partner?'' he interrupted sharply. ''Oh, for the love of Mike!''

Sierra clamped down on her anger. ''Sam is a well-respected custom farmer.''

''Farming is a very risky business, Sierra,'' Frank said disapprovingly.

"I understand that, but Sam knows what he's doing, and so do our backers."

Frank blinked at that. "Backers? This project actually has investors?"

"Not exactly. We took out a loan."

Frank rolled his eyes. "You're going to lose Tyree's whole future. Why can't you be reasonable? If you'd sell this place and move in with me, you could reinvest and make your money really grow."

"I'm not selling my home."

"Why do you need this house? Mine is large enough for all of us."

"I'm not selling my home."

"Fine. Lose it, then. That's what's going to happen."

Sierra put a hand to her head, where a dull ache had begun. "Dad, did you come here just to scold me, or was there another reason for your visit?"

He scowled, rammed his hands into his pockets and rocked back on his heels. "I'm concerned about my granddaughter. I called earlier, and Tyree said Dennis is taking her to lunch."

"Yes."

"He has no right to see her."

"He's her father."

"He doesn't pay his child support. He's just using her."

"I know that, and you know that, but Tyree doesn't."

"Then she needs to be told."

"For pity's sake, she's eight years old!" Sierra

erupted. "An eight-year-old cannot understand that her father isn't capable of loving her."

"Then keep him away from her! Take him to court if you have to."

"He's her father," she repeated forcefully. "All that will happen if I take him to court is that he'll be forced to pay his child support and my daughter will be even more angry with me than she is now when they also restrict his visits."

"Well, you have to do something!"

"I am! I'm doing my best to maintain my relationship with my daughter so if and when her manipulative jerk of a father shows his true colors I'll be able to help her overcome her disappointment and see that it has nothing to do with her."

Frank made an exasperated sound, "That's the most ridiculous idea I've ever heard. Keep him away from her." He shook his finger in her face. "If you had listened to me, none of this would be happening!"

Sierra hugged herself and said nothing, wondering if it never occurred to him that if she had listened to him, they wouldn't have Tyree to worry about or to love.

It was a difficult morning. Tyree had been glad to see her grandfather at first, but he made so many derogatory comments about Dennis that she was in a surly mood by the time he left, so she argued with Sierra about cleaning up her room before her father came. Sierra wound up threatening Tyree with losing television privileges for the evening if she didn't get her room straightened by the time Dennis arrived. Tyree was still up in her room banging things around and grumbling about having to do chores on Saturday when Dennis drove up to the house.

Sierra stepped out onto the front porch to have a word with him about the importance of him having Tyree home at the appointed time. The weather held bright and mild. The buzzing of a circular saw filled the air with the sound of progress. Sierra glanced toward the building site perhaps thirty yards away and saw that Sam had stripped down to his undershirt. He finished the cut just as Dennis got out of his car. Sam put aside the electric saw and brushed sawdust from his forearms and hair before peeling off the undershirt and shaking it out.

Sierra smiled. One thing she'd noticed about Sam since he'd started working here was his natural penchant for cleanliness and order. He never put away a tool without wiping it down, and he kept himself and his work site as clean as possible.

Footsteps crunched on gravel. Sierra turned to face Dennis and caught a disparaging look on his face.

"So that's the plowboy."

Sierra glared at him. Once Dennis had been handsome. Tall, dark, powerfully built, he had seemed manly and strong, someone who could stand against her father. Soon enough, however, his true weakness had been exposed, and now he seemed to wear it in every tired line on his face and the sag of muscles gone soft. She wasn't surprised that he'd heard about Sam, but he had some nerve speaking of him in that contemptuous manner.

"Don't call him that. He happens to be my business partner."

"Yeah? What's he plowing besides the field?" Dennis sneered.

Sierra's mouth fell open. "That's a filthy thing to say!"

"Oh, come on, Sierra. Everyone knows you've bought yourself a boy-toy."

"That's a lie!"

"You think I care if you're getting down and dirty with that kid? All that concerns me is what you're paying for it."

"That really is all you care about, isn't it, Dennis? The money. You can't bear the thought that someone else might get his hands on it!"

"I'm thinking about Tyree," he insisted. "It's her inheritance."

"Funny, you sure weren't concerned enough about Tyree to pay your child support when it was all I could do to keep a roof over her head. You weren't concerned about our daughter at all until I inherited a million bucks."

"That's not so. I just haven't been as lucky as you. I've had hard times."

"So have I."

"Well, I'm still having a hard time, but you just don't give a flip, do you?"

"Not even a little one."

"You are one cold b—"

"Don't think you can stand here and call me

filthy names on my own doorstep!'' she interrupted hotly.

''And some doorstep it is, too!''

''This doorstep is *mine,* Dennis. What does *yours* look like?''

''Oh, yeah, rub it in, why don't you? Money gets dumped in your lap, and I'm living hand-to-mouth. I get that, believe me!''

''Stop it!''

Sierra whirled around to find Tyree in the open doorway, her face contorted, tears streaming from her eyes.

''Stop it!'' she screamed again. ''Stop fighting! I hate you fighting!''

''Oh, honey, I'm sorry,'' Sierra began.

At the same moment, Dennis accused, ''Now look what you've done.''

''What I've done?'' Sierra exclaimed.

At that, Tyree tore across the porch and ran around the corner.

''Well, that's just terrific!'' Dennis shouted, throwing up his hands.

''Get out of here!'' Sierra told him angrily. ''I mean it, Dennis. Go!''

Dennis yanked open his car door. ''Fine. You've ruined the whole day, anyway!'' He dropped down behind the wheel and slammed the door. He was mouthing angry words as he drove away, but the window was up and the engine was running, and she didn't really care to hear it, anyway. She felt physically ill as she swung off the porch and around the house to go in search of her daughter. This was one day that surely couldn't get any worse.

Chapter Four

"Thank God!"

Sam turned from a giggling Tyree to her mother. He'd been hanging the first sheet of rigid plastic that would enclose the framework of the greenhouse when the girl had stumbled into him, sobbing. He'd caught her midfall, set her down, calmed her and teased a giggle out of her, but he still didn't know what the problem was. He wasn't surprised, however, that her mother had shown up.

"She's all right," he said encouragingly.

Sierra flashed him a wary look and focused once more on her daughter, who perched on a board laid across a pair of sawhorses. "I've looked all over for you."

To Sam's surprise, Tyree folded her arms and

stuck out her chin. She was a cute kid. Her hair was darker and not quite as curly as her mom's, but otherwise she looked just like a young Sierra sitting there. Sam hid a smile, bowing his head.

"I'm not talking to you," the child announced baldly.

Sam spoke from pure habit, using the same easy, no-nonsense tone that he employed with his sisters. "Hey, now, that's no way for a little girl to act. Your mom's obviously been worried about you."

Tyree's mulish expression intensified. "She was fighting with my daddy. I hate it when she fights with my daddy."

Sam shot a look at Sierra, who frowned guiltily. The sadness in her eyes pricked Sam's heart. "Yeah," Sam said to Tyree, "my parents used to fight, and I hated it, too, but you know what? Parents are just like kids sometimes. They get hurt and angry, too, and sometimes it spills out of their mouths without thinking. They're almost always sorry about it later."

Tyree glanced at her mother, then down at her hands. "Well, it hurts *my* feelings when they fight, so I don't want to talk to her."

"Uh-huh, the thing is, though, parents don't stop being parents even if they do act like kids sometimes, and kids don't get a pass on being respectful even when their parents behave like that." Tyree flattened her lips in a gesture of pure disgust, and Sam laughed. She was her mother's daughter. "Them's the world's rules, cupcake," he told her, chucking her under that Sierra chin. She sighed profoundly.

"Honey, I'm sorry," Sierra said, finally moving toward them. "Maybe your dad can take you to lunch tomorrow. Okay?"

"Okay," Tyree said grudgingly. "I guess I can give him his stuff then."

"Stuff?" Sierra echoed, and Sam heard the anger and dismay in her tone.

Tyree hopped down off the section of beam, saying smartly, "He doesn't have an Internet account. Why shouldn't I help him order his stuff?"

"Because he doesn't pay for the things you order for him, Tyree."

"So? He hasn't got any money, and we've got lots!"

"But what about his pride?" Sam interjected, shocked and alarmed by what he was hearing. "A man's got to have his pride, you know, and his pride's definitely going to sting if he lets his little girl pay for his stuff." Tyree looked troubled by that, so he pressed on. "He may not say so because he probably wouldn't want to hurt your feelings, and maybe he really needs the stuff, but deep down it's gotta sting. You know?"

Tyree bit her lip. Oh, man, her mom to her toenails, this one, which was good, since he was getting really bad vibes about her old man. What was it with some men? Tyree looked at her mom.

"I want to call him. Can I call him? Please?"

Sierra swallowed, then nodded. "Tell him to come tomorrow, okay?"

"Okay." With that Tyree turned and ran toward the house, her figure blurring as she moved behind the thick, colorless plastic.

Sierra pressed a hand to her forehead, then straightened and met his gaze. "Thank you."

He shrugged and looked away, but she drew his eyes back to her like metal shavings to a magnet. Even wearing a big, sloppy sweater and jeans with simple canvas shoes she looked sexy. She wandered a little closer, her shoes scuffing against the ground.

"I shouldn't have let him get to me," she said, "but Dennis doesn't care about Tyree. He doesn't care about anyone but himself."

Sam nodded. "Don't know the fellow, but if he's letting his eight-year-old buy him stuff over the Internet, he can't be what he should be, not in my book."

"Letting?" Sierra scoffed. "Encouraging is more like it."

He frowned at that but couldn't help asking, "What's a kid like her doing with Internet access, anyway?"

Sierra stiffened defensively. "The Internet is a valuable educational tool. All her friends have Internet access."

"So? I bet they're not using it to shop. What are you doing setting up accounts like that for her?"

"For books!" she exclaimed. "She's just supposed to buy books. We don't get the hot new kids' books out here because we don't have a bookstore in town."

"They can buy a lot more than books on those Web sites now."

"I know, but she's only supposed to buy books, and until her father showed up again, that's all she did buy."

Sam shook his head. "Kids shouldn't have that kind of purchasing power."

"She'd be fine if not for Dennis."

"I don't know. It seems a bit overboard for a little girl."

"Maybe it is," Sierra admitted ruefully.

He should have been satisfied with that, but no, he had to give that big old bear one more poke. "If I were you, I'd cancel the Internet service."

Predictably, Sierra lashed back. "Well, you're not me, and I won't deny my daughter one of her greatest pleasures just because her father can't be trusted! Besides, everyone has access to the Internet now."

"Not everyone," he said. "Kids can and do get along just fine without the Internet."

"Name one," Sierra retorted skeptically, "just one."

The words burned like acid in the back of his throat. "I'll name two. Keli and Kim Jayce."

Color blossomed in two spots high on her cheeks. "Oh. I—I didn't realize…that is, I didn't think before I spoke."

If that was her way of apologizing, he didn't want to hear it. "We find the public library real helpful. Maybe you ought to try it sometime. *They* get all the hot new kid books. I don't think my girls have missed a one.''

"Sam, I'm sorry. That was very thoughtless of me.''

"And they sure as heck don't go buying *stuff* off the Internet. Might as well give her a credit card and turn her loose in one of those mega malls in Dallas.''

Sierra jabbed her fists into the tops of her hips and glared at him. "Look, I've apologized for being insensitive, but one slip of the tongue doesn't give you the right to tell me how to raise my daughter.''

Too angry to think first, he drawled, "Well, somebody sure needs to.''

"Maybe so," she shot back, "but it won't be some wet-behind-the-ears kid with a sore spot!''

Kid. That word whirled inside his head. It was the same word he'd used for Tyree, and now Sierra was using it to describe him. But not for long.

"I'll show you wet-behind-the-ears," he muttered, striding toward her.

He didn't even know what he was about to do, didn't realize what he intended until he was reaching for her. He only knew that the man in him very much needed to make himself known to the woman in her, and the most direct way to do that was with a no-holds-barred kiss. He yanked her against him, fixed his lips to hers. At first, they stood frozen that way. Then, boom!

Heat exploded in that place, rushing down into his groin and melting her into him. He pressed his hands against her supple back, feeling the high, firm mounds of her breasts flatten against his chest. When her head fell back, he used that tiny break in the kiss to renegotiate the fit of their mouths. Her lips rose to meet his, and her arms slid around his torso. With an aching awareness he realized that she was every bit as engaged as he was. Bringing his hands to her face, he tilted her head, felt her mouth open beneath his and plunged his tongue inside, seeking a deeper connection.

Her hands closed in the back of his T-shirt, and she pushed her shoulders forward, molding her body against his. No age issue stood between them now. Whatever years separated their birth dates were no more significant in that moment than a snap of the fingers. They were man and woman, pure and simple, with a wild, hot desire growing at lightning speed between them.

A desire that should never, could never, be fulfilled.

Sam groaned, and for one insane moment he considered the possibility of throwing it all away. He could back right out of the partnership. It would take some doing, but it was possible. He could sever their financial ties. And then what? Ask an older, wealthier woman to give herself to a day laborer? That's what he would amount to if he crashed this deal. Maybe that was all he'd *ever* amount to if he crashed this deal.

Stepping back from that kiss required an impossible amount of willpower, but he managed it. For one long, heart-stopping moment after he disengaged, she stood just as if the kiss were going on, her face turned up, mouth ajar, eyes closed tight. She was the sweetest thing he'd ever seen, and he wanted her so badly that it stunned him, but a man in his position could do nothing except walk away.

So that's what he did.

Turning on his heel, he walked away as swiftly as he could. Their future—rather, their future*s,* since they had none together—depended on it.

When the telephone on her desk rang, Sierra jumped and stared at it with horror. What if it was Sam? After that devastating kiss, she hadn't been able to face him again. She still couldn't quite believe what had happened. One moment they'd been arguing and the next thing her toes were curling inside her shoes.

Everything had spun out of control then, and once her head had stopped going around and around, she'd found herself alone. She still felt scorched, branded, and she couldn't bear to imagine what he must be thinking. She, after all, was the mature one. At least that's what she'd tried to tell herself. Right now she wasn't so sure. Would a mature woman be afraid to speak to a man because he'd kissed her?

She snatched the phone from its cradle and answered in a very businesslike tone. "Sierra Carlton."

"Are you the Sierra Carlton who's in business with Sam Jayce?" a woman's voice asked.

Sierra couldn't decide whether to be alarmed or

relieved. On one hand, it wasn't Sam. On the other, it was *about* Sam. "Yes. May I ask who's calling?"

"My name is Lana Houston. I help Sam with his sisters' after-school care."

"Oh. Um, is there a problem? Some message you need me to pass to Sam?"

"It's a little more complicated than that, I'm afraid," Lana Houston said hesitantly. "The thing is, there's been an accident."

"Oh, no." The bottom dropped out of her stomach. Had something happened to Sam?

"Nothing too serious," Lana Houston hurried on. "Kim—one of the twins—has taken a fall, and she's going to need stitches."

Sierra practically wilted with relief, but stiffened with the recollection that a little girl was hurt, a little girl dear to Sam. "How can I help?"

"I need Sam here at the Urgent Care Center," Lana Houston told her. "The doctor won't touch her unless her legal guardian is here. I—I think it's because of the insurance situation. They don't have any, you see."

There had been a time when she and Tyree couldn't afford health-care insurance, but at least they'd had Frank to fall back on if the worst happened. Sam had no one but himself. And Lana Houston, apparently.

"It's not even lunchtime. Sam should still be at the farm."

"I've tried calling that number," Lana Houston said, "but no one answers."

"Yes, of course. I'm here, and Sam is working

outside. He wouldn't hear that phone. Doesn't he have a mobile number?''

"No. No, he doesn't."

"I'll go get him," Sierra decided aloud.

Lana Houston gushed with relief. "Oh, thank you. Thank you so much. I don't want to leave the girls."

"It may take a while. The farm's almost six miles out, and I'm not sure where Sam's working today."

"We'll be perfectly fine here until he comes," the Houston woman assured her. "Just knowing he's on his way will make Kim and Keli feel better, I'm sure."

"I'll be as quick as I can," Sierra said, reaching for her handbag.

A moment later, she was flying down the stairs and calling out to Bette to let her know that she was leaving. Ten minutes after that, she turned onto her own drive. In the distance she saw Sam climb down off the tractor in the field behind the house. She honked her horn and headed the car in his direction. By the time she'd reached the rough ground at the edge of the field, he was waiting for her. She hit a button and rolled down the passenger window. Sam bent and stuck his head inside.

"What's wrong?"

"They need you down at the Urgent Care Center. Kim fell. It's not serious, but she does need stitches."

His sage-green eyes deepened in color. "Where?"

"At school."

"No, I mean, where does she need the stitches? Where is she hurt?"

"I don't know. I didn't ask. A Lana Houston called and said they won't treat her unless you're there."

"Right." He straightened and looked around him as if hunting something. Seeming to find it, he bent down again. "Can you take me to my truck?"

"I'll do better than that," Sierra said, realizing that he was pretty shaken. "Get in and I'll take you to Kim."

He opened the door and dropped down into the seat. "Thanks. Hurry!" he said.

Sierra shifted the transmission into Reverse and backed the car around. As she placed the car in forward mode once more, Sam reached around and pulled his safety belt into place. Sierra concentrated on getting him to his sister as swiftly as possible while recounting for him her entire conversation with the mysterious Lana Houston. That didn't take long, and pretty soon Sam was shifting forward in his seat as if by doing so he could urge her to a faster speed. More to distract him than for any other reason, Sierra broached the topic of cell phones.

"I take it you don't have a mobile phone."

He flashed her a resentful glance and curtly informed her, "People can and do get along without them."

"Just like the Internet," she muttered, aware that she'd hit yet another nerve.

"Yeah. Just like that," he snapped, fidgeting in his seat again.

Sierra let the subject drop. When they pulled up in front of the Urgent Care Center, he was out of the car almost before it came to a stop and ran inside. Sierra bit her lip and decided to follow just in case a cooler head was needed. After parking, she went into the neat brick-and-glass building. When she inquired about Kim, the receptionist told her to go on back to room three and buzzed open the door for her. Sierra didn't argue or explain.

The room was already crowded with people when she arrived in the open doorway. She zeroed in on Sam, who stood next to the narrow cot, one arm wrapped around a slight child with short, pale blond hair who was parked on his hip. A similar child lay on the cot, and Sam bent over her, smoothing back her pale bangs as he pressed a kiss to her forehead.

"You okay, sugar? Where does it hurt?"

"It's her forearm," said the tall, shapely woman at his side.

Sierra recognized the voice, and her gaze went unerringly to its owner. Lana Houston looked to be in her early thirties with long, golden brown hair and unusual gray eyes rimmed in deep blue. She lifted one graceful hand to Sam's shoulder.

"So where's the doctor?" Sam wanted to know. "Why isn't he here?"

Lana Houston smiled, her wide, mobile mouth stretching into a knowing curve. "Relax. Kim's fine. I made sure they used a topical painkiller on the cut.''

Sam leaned down slightly and kissed her on the cheek. ''Thanks, Lana. What would I do without you?''

Sierra felt a stab of white-hot jealousy. It was that exact moment when Lana Houston turned and realized that Sierra was standing in the doorway.

''Oh. Hello.''

Sam looked over his shoulder, and his brow lifted in surprise. ''Sierra?''

She suddenly felt like an interloper. ''I—I just wanted to be sure she's okay.''

Lana Houston put out her hand, gliding swiftly across the floor. ''She's going to be just fine. Thank you so much for bringing Sam to us.''

To her horror, Sierra found that she couldn't summon up the same graciousness as the lovely Lana, so she merely nodded and allowed the other woman to squeeze her fingers.

''You haven't met the girls yet, have you?'' Lana went on. Reaching back, she laid a hand on Sam's shoulder, saying, ''Sammy, why don't you go see if you can locate that doctor, hmm? Meanwhile, I'll introduce the girls to Sierra.''

Sam nodded and set the girl he was holding onto her feet. He patted the shoulder of the other and promised to come right back. Then he slipped past Sierra into the hallway. Lana took each of the girls by the hand and made the introductions.

''This is Keli,'' she said, wagging the hand of the green-eyed, blond pixie Sam had been holding.

She smiled down at the girl on the bed. "And this is Kim, who caused all this excitement by falling off the slide at school."

The girls were virtually identical except for the cowlicks at the crowns of their heads. Like true mirror images of one another, their short, pale blond hair swirled in different directions and stood up on different sides of their heads. Of the two, Keli seemed the more reticent. She clutched Lana's hand tightly and stared up at Sierra with huge, soft green eyes a shade darker than Sam's, while her sister gave a jaunty little wave with her uninjured arm and voiced a strong "Hi."

"Hello."

"Girls, this is Ms. Carlton, Sam's new business partner."

"The flower lady," Kim said, and Lana smiled.

"Yes, the flower lady."

"I like flowers," Keli announced shyly.

"So do I," Sierra replied.

Sam returned then with the doctor, and Lana tugged Keli away from the bed, saying, "Let's step out and give the doctor room to work now."

Keli shook her head. "I want to stay with Kim."

Sam smoothed a hand over the back of her head. "No, sweetie, you go with Lana and Sierra. This room's too little for all of us. I'll stay with Kim and make sure she's all right. We won't be long, I promise."

"But my arm hurts, too," she persisted.

"I know it does, angel, but it'll feel better as soon as Kim does. The best thing is for us all to just let the doc do his thing and make you both well. Okay?''

Kim lifted her head then and said, "It's all right, Keli. I'm not scared."

Keli bowed her head and let Lana ease her from the room. Sam's attention was already claimed by the child on the bed.

"She's a little scared," Keli whispered.

"Of course she is," Lana said matter-of-factly, "but she'll be fine." She looked at Sierra and said, "There's a waiting room down this hall. We'll go there."

"All right."

They started walking sedately in that direction, Keli dragging her feet at Lana's side and occasionally looking over her shoulder.

"They're very empathetic with one another," Lana explained softly. "I don't know that they actually experience each other's pain and emotions, but they're very sensitive to what the other is feeling."

"I've heard of that sort of thing with twins," Sierra said, interested.

Lana nodded and herded Keli through the door into the small waiting room, where a television played quietly even though the room was empty. Lana leaned her shoulder against the wall beside the doorway and said, "Sam was always very sensitive, too. I remember when he first came to us his mother would call on the phone, and she'd sound perfectly normal to me. Then the two of them would chat for a few minutes and Sam would hang up and say, 'She's been hurt again,' or 'She's worried.' He just knew somehow.''

Sierra digested that, then asked, ''When he first came to you?''

Lana glanced at her with undisguised surprise. ''Sam used to live with us.''

''Us?''

''My husband Chet and I. We were Sam's foster parents at one time.''

Foster parents? Sierra thought, stunned. ''But you're so young.''

Lana laughed, the sound wafting musically through the hall. ''Not as young as you might think. Let's just say I won't see forty again.''

Sierra's jaw dropped. ''I'd have said thirty! I actually thought that maybe you and Sam were...'' She blushed at what she'd thought.

It was Lana's turn to gape. ''Not hardly. Sam's like a son to us. Of all the children we've fostered, we're closer to Sam than any of the others.'' She folded her arms and declared ruefully, ''Frankly, I'd be delighted if Sam had a woman in his life, but he won't take time for dating. He's too fixated on these girls, and when he's not with them, he's busy earning a living.''

Sierra shrugged. ''I know how it is,'' she admitted. ''I'm a single parent myself. I'm sure Sam has even less time to socialize than I do.''

Lana sighed. ''Well, if you ask me, it isn't healthy. Young people like you and Sam should get out and enjoy yourselves once in a while, find someone to share your lives with.''

"Oh, I don't know about that," Sierra hedged. "I tried that route once, and the experience doesn't exactly encourage me to make a return trip."

Lana tilted her head and said gently, "Everyone has bad experiences, but the strong ones get past them. I want a strong girl for Sam because he needs someone who can be as strong for him as he's always been for everyone else. He's played nursemaid enough in his life."

Sierra nodded, murmuring, "I'm sure the right girl is out there for Sam."

"I hope so," Lana Houston said, "because our Sam is quite a catch. He'll make some lucky woman a wonderful husband. He's already proven to be an excellent father, and he deserves children of his own someday. Unfortunately, we don't always get what we deserve in this life." She straightened away from the wall, looked at Keli playing quietly with some beat-up toys left in the waiting room and added softly, "Then again, sometimes we do."

Sierra stayed where she was, watching as Lana Houston dropped to the floor and happily joined in Keli's play. An unusual woman, to say the least. She seemed very good with the girls; she must've been good for Sam, too. They made an odd family of sorts, but no odder, Sierra supposed, than her own, and a good deal more supportive. A new envy assailed her. She wallowed in it for a moment, then allowed it to pass as she hovered there on the periphery. On the outside.

Chapter Five

"I'm surprised you're still here."

Sam stood in the waiting room door, holding
Kim, whose left arm had been bandaged and placed
in a sling. Sierra sat in a straight-backed chair next
to Keli, holding a children's book from which she
had apparently been reading aloud. Keli apparently
hadn't told her that, at seven, she and her sister both
could read as well as or even better than any ten-
year-old. Sierra looked at Sam now with studied
indifference.

"Lana was called away by Child Welfare Ser-
vices. I told her I'd get you and the girls where you
need to go."

Sam sighed inwardly. He'd been hoping to avoid
this. It was one thing to ride into town with her

when his mind was clouded with worry; it was another thing entirely once the crisis was past. He couldn't help noticing how trim and cool she looked in slim turquoise slacks and a matching cowl-necked sweater and jacket with her hair swept up in a neat roll on the back of her head. Curls had sprung up around her face, and a very pretty face it was. He'd mentally kissed that face a thousand times a night since he'd been stupid enough to kiss it in fact.

"My truck's at your place," he said, "so I guess that's where we better get."

Nodding, Sierra rose, and Keli rose with her. As they moved out into the hall, Kim smiled at her sister and announced, "It hardly hurts at all."

Kim giggled and continued, "Sam gagged and got dizzy, but he was just joshing to keep me from looking at the doctor poke in the needle."

"Heck, she was braver than me," Sam insisted. "She's so tough I could've sewed her up with my hemming needle and thread off the spool."

"Uh-uh, not the way you sew!" Kim exclaimed, laughing as Sam carried her toward the exit.

Keli chortled as she followed, saying to Sierra, "Once Sammy sewed up Kimmy's blue puppy dog with black thread. It was icky!"

"Bluebell's not icky," Kim protested.

"No, but Sam's sewing is!" Keli joked. Both girls laughed gaily.

"Hey!" Sam said, pretending offense, "Old Bluebell's still holding his stuffing, isn't he?"

"We tied a ribbon 'round the icky stitching," Kim divulged over his shoulder.

Keli snickered, and Sam turned to find Sierra holding Keli's hand, her eyes dancing with laughter, as well. His heart gave a strange kick, but he supposed it was a natural aftereffect of the panic he had felt at hearing one of the girls was injured. Stitches. He'd felt sicker at the sight of his baby sister getting sewed up than he'd ever admit. He held Kim a little tighter at the memory of it.

He had a bad moment at the receptionist's desk when he had to explain that he could only pay half of the charges and the remainder would be paid out in installments. They'd be eating macaroni and cheese for a while. He hadn't wanted Sierra to hear that part and was much relieved when she offered to go bring the car around while he took care of it.

True to form, Keli stuck right by him, standing pressed against his leg while Kim rode the other hip. Then when he was tucking the folded receipt into his pocket, Keli looked up at him and said, "Ms. Carlson's real nice."

Sam smiled and nodded, cupping the back of her head with one hand as he moved them all toward the front door and the sidewalk beyond.

"She's got a little girl named Tyree," Keli divulged importantly.

"I know her," Kim said. "Tyree. She's that rich girl two grades up."

Keli's eyes grew even larger. "They're rich?"

"Some people might think so," Sam muttered, watching Sierra's expensive luxury sedan pull up to the curb, "but it's not a polite topic for conversation. Understand?"

Both girls nodded. Smiling, Sam ushered them toward Sierra's car, opened the rear door and belted them both into their seats before walking around and taking the passenger seat next to Sierra.

"Do you mind if I swing by the school and pick up Tyree on the way?" Sierra asked, driving away from the clinic. "It's a little early, but I'll be late if I have to drive out to the farm and back first."

"No problem," Sam said. "I can pick up Kim's assignments for the next couple days. Doc says she can't go back until Monday."

"Lana said to tell you that it wouldn't be a problem if Kim needs to stay with her for a while." Sierra looked into the rearview mirror and said to Kim, "There's a baby coming to stay with Lana and Chet."

"A baby!" Kim gushed.

"Oh, boy!" Keli exclaimed.

Sam chuckled. "They love a baby almost as much as Lana does, and Lana loves the babies best. She loves all the kids, but she absolutely delights in the babies, and let me tell you, some of them are pretty pitiful." He shook his head.

"Has she had many foster children?" Sierra asked.

"Hundreds," Sam answered. "Me included."

"She told me. It takes a special person to be a foster parent."

"Especially the way Lana and Chet do it," Sam

said. "They pour their whole hearts into every child—and then let them go."

"I don't know how they manage that."

"Special people, like you said," Sam told her. "God knows they saved my life in more ways than one."

"What do you mean?"

"For one thing," Sam said carefully, aware of the girls in the back seat, "I saw a whole different sort of man in Chet than I'd ever seen before, a man as good as he is strong, and for another…let's just say they kept me out of harm's way."

Sierra smiled and glanced in his direction, saying softly, "I'm glad."

Sam felt his heart give that funny little kick again, but he ignored it, turning his gaze out the window as he muttered, "Yeah, me, too."

They made the remainder of the drive out to the school in silence, except for the girls whispering and giggling in the back seat. Sierra parked in the pickup lane behind one other vehicle while Sam went inside to report on Kim's condition and briefly speak to her teacher. When he came out again, hauling Kim's backpack with her books and assignments inside, Tyree was waiting with the others. All three girls were laughing and talking a mile a minute.

Sam couldn't help noticing that his sisters looked a little shabby in their knit pants, T-shirts, bulky sweaters and canvas shoes, compared to Tyree's plaid slacks, shiny blouse, pink vinyl jacket with white piping and matching blunt-toed shoes with open heels. She looked like something out of a little girl's fashion magazine with her long, dark red hair caught up in a frothy pink bow, while Kim and Keli resembled a pair of ragamuffins—cute little ragamuffins—but ragamuffins, nonetheless. He told himself that it didn't matter. The girls were happy. Even Kim, sporting six stitches in her left forearm, was laughing and giggling with the others.

He shouldn't have been surprised when they reached the farm and Tyree begged for the girls to be allowed to come inside and play for a while.

"Oh, I don't know," Sam hedged, torn between personally protecting Kim and the tractor sitting in the field.

"I'll keep a close eye on them, especially our patient here," Sierra pledged.

"Please, Sammy," Kim begged.

"Please, Sammy," Keli echoed.

"Please, please, please," Tyree added.

Finally, he gave in. "Okay, long as you're not too rambunctious." He smoothed Kim's cowlick and cautioned, "I wouldn't want to explain to the doc how you busted those stitches open." The probability of that was actually quite small. The doc had said that infection was the only real concern, but that was minimal, too.

"I'll be careful," Kim promised.

"We'll all be careful," Tyree said.

"Guess I'll do a little work then," Sam said as the girls hurried into the house.

"Take as much time as you need," Sierra told him, following behind the girls.

It would be good, he decided, to finish up what he'd started when he'd been interrupted. Why, then, did he feel as if he'd just turned some important corner?

"Good chicken," Kim said, shoving another bite into her mouth.

Sierra smiled. "Glad you like it."

"Mom's a good cook," Tyree said, waving a green bean around on the end of her fork.

"Uh-huh," Keli agreed, loading her spoon with rice swimming in gravy. "Sammy just cooks rice for breakfast with syrup."

"Syrup?" Tyree chirped. "Yuck!"

"It's good," Kim insisted. Then she smiled at Sierra. "But this is better."

"Thank you," Sierra said.

"But let's not tell Sam," Keli said in conspiratorial tone.

"Tell Sam what?"

Sierra looked up to find Sam standing in the kitchen door. He looked tired and dusty and man enough to rope the moon. His sisters certainly thought he'd hung it. Sierra got up and went for the tumbler of ice she'd stowed in the freezer.

"That supper's ready," she answered smoothly. "Do you take tea?"

"You bet." He surveyed the table and the girls ranged around it, then turned back to the kitchen as she slipped past him. "Didn't mean to be so late."

"No problem." She took the tumbler from the

freezer and filled it with tea from the pitcher on the kitchen island.

"Thanks for feeding the girls."

"My pleasure." She walked to the double-wall oven and turned off the warmer before taking up a hot pad and reaching inside for the plate she'd put back for him. "You can wash up in the sink."

He moved hesitantly to the sink and began soaping his hands. "Wasn't expecting dinner," he said carefully.

She smiled at him over her shoulder as she carried his plate and glass to the table. "The girls were hungry."

He nodded and rinsed off. It seemed to take him an inordinately long time to dry his hands, remove his cap and walk to the table.

"Sorry for just walking in," he apologized, lowering himself onto the chair. "I did knock at the laundry room door first."

"No problem," Sierra said lightly. "I guess we didn't hear you."

He picked up his knife and fork and cut into the boneless, pan-grilled chicken breast. Winking at the girls he teased, "I know what happened. Ya'll were talking at once with your mouths full probably."

"Uh-uh," Tyree refuted automatically, then realizing that she had food in her mouth, she clamped a hand over it, much to the amusement of Kim and Keli, who nearly fell out of their chairs laughing.

Sam grinned and forked up a bite of chicken. "Mmm." He chewed and swallowed. "Beats those beans and wieners I was planning."

"Eewww!" Kim and Keli cried in unison.

Sam put on a frown for effect and said to Sierra, "For some strange reason they don't seem to like my beans and wieners."

Sierra laughed as Kim launched into a vivid explanation of why they'd starve before they'd eat Sam's beans and wieners again—a concoction of salt, mustard, ketchup, beans and big, big hunks of onion and wieners burned so black that they crumbled. Sam just grinned and placidly concentrated on eating. Sierra had heaped his plate high, and before he was done, Tyree got up and suggested to the girls that they run back upstairs and play some more before they had to go, but the twins looked to Sam for permission before so much as budging from their chairs. He shook his head.

"You know the rules."

Quick as bunnies the twins hopped up and began clearing the table, even Kim with her injured arm. Tyree flashed a surprised look at Sierra, then pitched in, taking a plate from Kim. Sierra felt torn between irritation and pleased surprise.

"They really don't have to help clean up," she began, but Sam lifted a hand.

"Yes, they do. That's how it's done at our house. Somebody cooks for them, they help clean. That way everybody contributes and everybody feels good about themselves. Lana and Chet taught me the importance of that."

Sierra gulped. She'd never thought of it that way. She'd always thought she was sparing Tyree unpleasantness by not insisting that she help clean up.

That couldn't be why Tyree always balked at picking up after herself, could it?

Sierra had the answer to that a few moments later when the girls returned from the kitchen and Sam said, "Better get on about clearing away your toys. We have to go soon."

Kim and Keli started happily scampering away. Only Tyree remained to sullenly argue. "Can't they stay a little longer? We're not through having fun yet."

"No, ma'am," Sam replied evenly. "The girls have homework to do and baths to take before bedtime."

"Well, when can they come back?" she wanted to know.

"I'll discuss that with your mom."

"Soon. Pleease," Tyree wheedled. "Tomorrow!"

"Not tomorrow," Sam said, "but before long."

"Mom!" Tyree protested.

"Come on, Tyree," Kim said, coming back to snag Tyree by the hand.

"But—"

"Come on," Kim insisted, tugging on Tyree's hand. Reluctantly, Tyree allowed herself to be towed toward the doorway. Embarrassed by her daughter's persistence—why hadn't she realized how poor Tyree's manners were?—Sierra kept her mouth shut. Abruptly, Tyree dug in her heels, though, and turned back.

"They can come to my birthday party, can't

they? I want them to come to my birthday party. Please, Mom. Make him say yes.''

Sierra glanced at Sam uncomfortably. ''It's not until the end of March.''

''We'll see,'' Sam said, noncommittal.

Tyree stuck out her chin, but before she could open her mouth to argue again, Kim and Keli took her by the arms and literally propelled her toward the doorway, whispering fiercely. To Sierra's relief, Tyree went along without another word.

''I'm sorry,'' Sierra began. Sam resumed eating. ''She's not usually so…''

''Demanding,'' he supplied after a moment.

Sierra felt a spurt of indignation. ''Tyree hasn't had the influence of a father.''

''And my girls haven't had the influence of a mother,'' Sam said matter-of-factly. ''You wouldn't be saying dads are more important than moms, would you?'' Sierra opened her mouth. Then closed it again. ''I didn't think so.'' He set aside his fork and folded his arms against the edge of the table, regarding her frankly. ''Look, I'm not trying to tell you how to raise your daughter. Your rules are your rules, and mine are mine, but *my* girls obey *my* rules. Okay?''

Sierra nodded mutely. He picked up his fork and swiftly, systematically cleaned his plate. Sierra left him to it, loading the washer with the rinsed dishes that the girls had stacked in the sink. She came to some conclusions while she did that. His rules seemed to work better than hers. Kim and Keli were delightful. She walked back into the breakfast room drying her hands on a damp dish towel.

He cleaned his plate and drained his glass of the last drop of tea. When he set the tumbler down onto the corner of the place mat and leaned back in his chair with a sigh, she asked, quite sincerely, "How'd you get so smart?"

His mouth quirked up on one end. "I went to a good school. That would be the school of hard knocks. Heard of it?"

Sierra chuckled silently and shook her head. "Speaking of school, I was thinking I could pick up the girls from school one day next week when I pick up Tyree, if that's all right with you. I promise we'll play by your rules."

He shrugged, but he was grinning. "How about Tuesday? Kimmy gets her stitches out on Wednesday, and Lana takes them to the library on Thursdays."

"Tuesday it is."

"I'll have the school put your name on the pickup list."

"Okay. Yeah, do that."

"All right then." He got up, placed his utensils on his plate and carried it, along with the iced tea glass, to the kitchen sink. He rinsed the dishes and left everything on the counter. Sierra just watched, liking the easy way he moved around the place. Sam Jayce, she mused, was a man very comfortable in his own skin. He was not, however, so comfortable alone with her.

She wondered if he would mention the kiss, or

if he might even repeat it. He turned his back to the counter and leaned against it, his arms spread out and compactly muscled hands resting lightly on the edge of the countertop behind him. Her heart sped up. Broad-shouldered, slim-hipped, long-limbed, Sam Jayce was a potent hunk of young man, even dusty and sweat-stained.

"That was a mighty fine dinner, Sierra. We don't usually eat so good."

"Thank you."

"No. Thank you. For everything. For coming after me, for hanging around the clinic when Lana got called away, for putting up with the girls. Dinner, of course."

"You're welcome, Sam," she told him. "As for the girls, we enjoyed having them here. You, too. It just feels…right."

As soon as the words were out, she knew it was the wrong thing to say, the exact wrong thing to say. He straightened away from the counter, rubbed his hands against his thighs, caught his breath, frowned, smiled, caught his breath again. "Well, we better get going. You want to call the girls down? Or maybe I should just go up and get them."

"No, I'll have them come down," she said, crossing the room to the intercom recessed above a small built-in desk. She flipped a switch and pushed a button, speaking into a small microphone grate. "It's time to go, girls. Come down to the kitchen, please."

A second later, Tyree's plaintive voice came through the system. "Mooom."

"Right now," Sierra said firmly. "Sam's waiting." She turned off the mike and turned a wryly apologetic smile at Sam.

"Man, they've got some wild gadgets these days," he muttered, glancing at the intercom. Sierra just nodded. "I figure most of it's more trouble than it's worth," he went on, then blinked and added, "That, uh, seems useful, though."

"It's handy in a house this big," she said, intensely aware of the tension.

He looked like he wanted to crawl into a cupboard. Several awkward moments later, the girls came into the kitchen chattering. The twins flanked Sam, and Tyree came straight to Sierra, a pleading expression on her face. Before Tyree could beg for more time, Sierra slipped an arm around her shoulders and informed her that the girls could come over again on Tuesday.

"Cool," Kim announced, sliding her injured arm into the sling hanging loose about her neck.

"Can I bring my baby doll, Sam?" Keli asked, looking up at him.

"Sure, sweetie. Now what do you say to Ms. Carlton?"

"Sierra, please," she corrected, looking to Sam, "if that's permissible."

Sam looked uneasy, but he acquiesced. "What do you say to Sierra?"

"Thank you. We had a very nice time," the twins chorused.

"And dinner was real good," Kim added.

Keli glanced up at Sam, qualifying anxiously, "You cook as good as Sam."

Sam laughed at that. "She cooks a whole lot better than me, sweetie, and I'm not a bit shy of saying it." He nodded at Sierra and herded the girls toward the back door. "Thanks again. Good night."

"See you Tuesday!" Tyree called as they all trooped to the back door.

"I'll bring my baby doll!" Keli promised.

When they were gone, Tyree looked up at her mother and said, "Maybe I ought to get a baby doll."

Sierra blinked in surprise. It had been years since Tyree had played with anything but those grownup teen dolls. "I thought you didn't like baby dolls."

Tyree shrugged. "They're okay sometimes."

Sierra smiled. "Maybe for your birthday then."

"Not before that?" Tyree whined. "Come on, Mom."

"Maybe for your birthday," Sierra repeated, smoothing her dark hair back from her face. "Meanwhile, maybe Keli will let you play with hers if you're nice."

Tyree blew a disgusted breath through her nose. Then she looked up at her mother and said. "I like them."

"So do I."

"You like him?"

Sierra sharpened her gaze. "Sam?" Tyree nodded. Sierra considered putting her off with a shrug or an offhanded remark, but something told her that it was important to be scrupulously honest in this, with herself as much as with Tyree. She nodded and said gently, "Very much."

"Did you know that their daddy killed their mother?" Tyree asked then.

Sierra masked her surprise. "Yes."

"Because he was drunk," Tyree went on matter-of-factly, "but they don't remember it. Sam had to tell them 'cause some kids were talking about it at school. It's okay, though, 'cause Sam takes good care of them."

"I'm sure he does."

Tyree screwed up her face and asked bluntly, "Daddy wouldn't do nothing to kill you. Would he?"

"No," Sierra answered firmly. "No, he wouldn't. We may not get along, but neither of us would ever do anything like that."

"I didn't think so," Tyree said confidently.

Sierra just smiled and hugged her daughter. For the first time in a long while she had reason to be thankful that Dennis Carlton was Tyree's father. She could've done worse, after all.

She looked at the dishes Sam had stacked on her countertop thoughtfully.

She could've done worse, but she also could have done better.

Chapter Six

"Holy cow, it's three supermodels!"

The girls giggled at Sam's outrageous comment. Tyree whirled the end of the pink feather boa she was wearing with a black strapless "evening gown" which was in reality one of her mother's long skirts. Kim hunched her shoulders and smooched the air with hot-pink lips, the strap of Sierra's ivory camisole falling down almost to her waist. Cobbled together with her own rolled-up knit pants, white socks and black high heels, the lacy camisole made for one weird getup. Keli stuck one hand behind her head and posed with her nose pointing toward the ceiling. She had belted a navy blue satin blouse of Sierra's with an orange sash and carried a matching orange handbag that clashed violently with Sierra's bright red high heels.

Sam perched on the edge of Sierra's den sofa and opened his arms. The twins crawled onto his knees as well as their clothing would let them, while Tyree plopped down onto the floor in front of him. He kissed the cheeks of the twins and patted Tyree's.

"Looks like you emptied your mom's closet."

"Not hardly!" Tyree exclaimed, and Sam lifted a brow at a grinning Sierra. She just shrugged unrepentantly. Well, he supposed that most women liked clothes. He couldn't really hold it against her. As for himself, he tried to keep enough jeans, T-shirts, underwear and socks to make it through the week without a wash.

"Now listen here, I don't want ya'll leaving the house like this," Sam told the girls with mock sincerity. "Some photographer sees you, he's liable to chase you down the street, thinking you're someone famous."

Kim rolled her eyes, scolding, "Sammy!" Keli clapped her hands over her mouth, giggling, while Tyree put on her "big girl" disdain with a huff, but she couldn't keep the grin off her face.

"I mean it," Sam teased, deadpan. "Ya'll go out looking like that and boys are going to want to kiss you, and we can't have that for, oh, ten years, at least."

Keli made gagging sounds. Tyree smacked herself in the forehead and exclaimed, "Oh, brother!" Kim, however, got a cagey look.

"I've already been kissed," she announced.

Sam knew this story in detail. Jeremy McPherson, all of five years old, had been fascinated with the twins in kindergarten, and one day he'd chased them until he'd caught Kim and kissed her. The girls had thought it "gross" and hilariously funny. It occasionally came up again. This time he pretended not to remember.

"Is that so? Guess it's time to head for the hills, then."

"What hills?" Tyree wanted to know.

"Oh, they've got some tall hills out west of the Pecos," Sam told her. "I've got one all picked out. It's got plenty of boulders to roll down on the boys when they come calling."

Tyree clapped her hands to her head. "You can't do that!"

"I can't?"

The girls all doubled up with laughter. "No!"

Sam sighed and flattened his lips in a show of disgust. "Well, shoot. I guess I'll have to let you gals date one of these days."

"Yes!"

"I figure thirty's about the right age."

"No!"

"Fourteen!" Tyree asserted.

"Try sixteen, cupcake, *if* you dress like an old lady on her way to church."

"Sam!"

"Sixteen and not a day before," he insisted.

Tyree jumped up and threw her arms around his neck to knock him over. All three girls mobbed him. He laughed and, despite the fact that he was dusty and sweaty, reached around all three of them, squeezing until they begged for mercy and Sierra intervened.

"Time to get cleaned up for supper. Go on now. It's almost on the table."

The girls bounced up and tottered away in too-big shoes, giggling. They sure enjoyed one another's company. He looked at his hands. They weren't obviously soiled, but he knew he needed to wash up. Before he could make a move to do so, however, Sierra dropped down onto the sofa next to him. He'd noticed when he'd come in that she was wearing black pants that stopped short of her ankles and hugged her slender curves like second skin along with a matching, long-sleeved turtleneck with cutouts that left her shoulders bare. Clothes like that definitely made a man think about what lay beneath them. Hoping to derail that train of thought, he hung his forearms on his knees and tried not to look at her.

"You are so good with those girls," she said.

"It's really just that I like being around them, you know. Tyree included."

"That's obvious."

"I have to thank you, Sierra, for having the twins over so often. I get to spend a-more time with them this way, and Lana's load gets lightened a bit, too."

"We love having them here. You know that. Tyree adores being the big girl in the group, but the truth is that Kim and Keli are a good influence on her. Even her father has mentioned how much happier she seems lately."

"That's real nice," Sam said, "but you shouldn't think that you have to keep cooking for us all the time."

Sierra crossed her legs. Her foot, in its soft, little black slipper, rubbed against his shin as she did so. The temperature seemed to shoot up about ten degrees. "Well, of course I don't," she was saying. "You're not here all the time."

Suddenly feeling dry-mouthed, Sam licked his lips. "I mean on the days the twins are here, you don't have to cook for us."

"I like cooking for you. It's more fun than just Tyree and I eating alone together. Of course, if you don't like my cooking..." She uncrossed her legs as if she meant to get up. Before he even knew he was going to do it, he dropped a hand onto her knee to keep her in place. Heat jolted up his arm. He took his hand away, careful not to snatch it back.

"You know that's not it. We've never eaten so well as we do here. But we don't want to take advantage."

"Okay. Tell you what, I'll make a deal with you." She leaned forward, matching his posture, and bumped her shoulder into his. "I'll only cook when I really want to. How's that?"

He chuckled. She had him pretty neatly boxed in. "I don't suppose you'd consider letting me buy groceries on occasion then?"

"Sure. If you want something special."

He turned his head to look at her. "And what would that be?"

She slipped her arm through his. "You tell me."

He couldn't have told her his name just then, not with her sitting so close. They were practically nose to nose, close enough that a mere tilt of his head would have resulted in a kiss. A kiss he wanted very badly. He tried to remember all the reasons it was not a good idea. When he got to money, he finally recognized the looming disaster. Gulping, he sat back.

"I'll, uh, have to give it some thought."

"Okay," she said, popping up onto her feet. "Why don't you get washed up so you can help me set the table?"

"Sure. Yeah. Uh-huh."

Sam couldn't *not* watch as she pivoted and walked away, if that hip-swaying slink could be called walking. Sam closed his eyes, feeling singed around the edges. Well, that's what happened when you played with fire. Good grief, how had he let this happen? Sierra Carlton was the very last woman with whom he should be spending time. Yet here he was. Again. She was getting to be a bad habit. Yet, the evenings that he and the girls didn't spend here with Sierra and Tyree seemed strangely flat and incomplete now.

He tried to think of her as his business partner, maybe even a friend. Instead he kept dreaming about putting his hands on her, laying his mouth against the long, graceful column of her throat and hearing her cry out as he pushed into her.

Oh, man. What was he doing? And why couldn't he stop?

* * *

Sam squirted the girls with the sink sprayer, splattering the kitchen floor and island. Shrieking, they put up their hands and fell, laughing, against the counters. Tyree had the presence of mind to hold up the dish towel she'd been using to dry the pot lids, so Sam snatched it and sprayed her again. Tyree screamed and laughed so hard that she bumped into Keli, who stumbled and went down on a wet patch of floor vinyl. Sam dropped the sprayer and somehow managed to catch her before she hit something. The sprayer, however, hit the edge of the sink, showering Sierra, who thought she'd found a safe spot in the corner of the counter.

She caught her breath, wet from the top of her head to her waist in front, and realized that everyone had stopped laughing. Grabbing a discarded dish towel from the countertop, she silently mopped her face then made a grab for the sprayer and, to the vast amusement of the girls, drenched Sam before he could wrestle it away from her. Arms, elbows and hands flying, knees and feet bumping, bodies twisting and writhing, they grappled with the chrome head attached to several feet of narrow rubber hose, laughing uproariously all the time.

Finally—and quite unfairly, she thought, given his superior strength—he succeeded in gaining control of the sprayer and shutting off the water supply. Then it was just the girls laughing as the two adults became fully aware of their situation.

They were standing against the sink, bodies plastered together, arms entwined. They blinked at each other, and then Sierra felt his pulse quicken and elation soared within her. She had suspected that he, too, had been feeling the electricity that crackled so often between them since that kiss, but for weeks now she'd waited for some definite proof. Finally, she had it.

Sam immediately detangled himself and started grabbing towels to mop up the water. Sierra shoved damp hair out of her face and smiled at the girls.

"Grab some more towels, kids, and let's mop up."

"No!" Sam said, holding the dishcloths in front of him. Four pairs of very surprised, curious eyes fell on him. "Uh, my fault. I'll clean up by myself."

"Oh, that's okay," Sierra said, tilting her head. "We all shared in the fun."

"I insist." His tone was light, but the look he fixed on her was determined.

She was pretty sure she understood the problem. She had felt it lengthening against her belly. Spreading her arms wide, she stepped in front of him and shooed the girls toward the door. "All gigglers into the den."

Living up to the description, the girls bounced and skipped and hopped from the room. They never *walked* anywhere, those three, and it was a complete delight to watch. Sierra cast a look over her shoulder as she followed the girls. Sam stood with the dish towels dangling from his hands, head bowed as if contemplating the task ahead. She wanted to tell him how wonderful he was, how much he thrilled her. She wanted to let him how much his and the twins being here meant to her.

Tyree never seemed happier than she did when he and the twins were around. They were darlings, both of them, so easy to love, and Sierra wanted to believe that she added something important to their lives, just as Sam seemed to bring something important to Tyree's. She and Tyree still had their difficult moments, of course, usually after Tyree had spent time with her father, but Sam and the twins provided a very welcome distraction from that old war. It was almost as if they were a family, she and Sam and the girls. Almost.

Turning away, Sierra followed the girls. Now that she knew Sam felt the attraction as keenly as she did, she had to accept the fact that he was obviously fighting it. Why? The age thing, of course. The five, almost six, years between them had seemed quite a gulf to her, too, in the beginning, but Sam had proved he was mature far beyond his years. How could she convince him she wasn't too old?

They already spent a couple of hours two or three evenings a week together, but the girls were always part of that, a huge part. Well, she'd take what she could get for the moment. Maybe an opportunity would present itself…eventually. Or she could sit him down and have a frank talk with him. She imagined how such a conversation might go.

"I've come to see what a wonderful man you are, Sam, and I'm just wild about you."

"No kidding? You mean it? Because I'm nuts

about you, too. I just never thought you'd be inter-
ested in me."

"More than interested. Make love to me."

Then the girls would run screaming into the
room, and that would be that. Shaking her head
wryly, she plopped down onto the couch, plucked
her damp shirt away from her body and set her
mind to dreaming up some other way to get him
alone, vaguely aware that the girls were going
through the DVDs that had arrived that afternoon
in the mail from the movie club to which she sub-
scribed. When Sam came into the room, rolling
down his sleeves, Sierra was no closer to solving
her problem. She sat up straighter and smiled in
what she hoped was a beguiling fashion. He probably thought she was grinning at the wet spots on
his clothing.

Whatever he thought, he ignored her and spoke
to the twins. "Ready to go?"

"Oh, Sammy, look!" Kim exclaimed, bouncing
up from the floor with a DVD case in hand. "It's
the wizard movie! Can we watch it? Oh, please,
please. There's no school tomorrow."

"It's true," Sierra supplied helpfully. "Tomorrow's a teacher workday, so the girls have a long
weekend."

"I know. That's why Lana has planned an outing
tomorrow," Sam said. "Besides, I really need to
get on home and take a shower."

"But you're all wet already!" Tyree pointed out.

"A *real* shower," Sam amended.

"Oh, Sammy, please," Keli pleaded. "We've waited and waited to see it."

"It won't be in the rental shops for another month," Sierra added. Sam shot her a killing glare. "I tell you what, the girls can take it home with them."

"Mooom!" Tyree protested.

"You saw it at the theater," Sierra reminded her.

"We don't have a DVD player," Sam said flatly, "and I need a shower."

Kim and Keli had subsided, and Kim now dropped the DVD on the floor. The pair of them stared at it morosely but said not another word. Sam grimaced.

"All right. I spend ninety percent of my time covered in grit anyway." The girls brightened visibly, but Sam was clearly unhappy.

"If I might make another suggestion," Sierra ventured cautiously. He crooked an eyebrow at her, his expression stating that she'd done quite enough for one evening. She took a deep breath. "Why don't you go on home and have a nice long shower? The girls can spend the night here."

"Yeah!" Tyree agreed.

"No," Sam said, holding up one hand to forestall further argument. "Lana's made plans, and she's expecting them early tomorrow morning."

"Well, then I'll run them home as soon as the movie's over."

Sam's face clouded. "I'll come back for them," he said implacably.

"You don't have to do that," Sierra began, but

he glared her into silence, bringing his hands to hips.

"I said I'll come back for them, and that's final."

Stung, Sierra tucked her hands beneath her thighs and looked away. "Fine."

He stood there a moment, then mumbled, "No reason you should have to get Tyree out so late."

Sierra tried to smile, but she couldn't help wondering why he had to be so testy at times. They'd had so much fun earlier. Everyone had been so happy. Maybe he was attracted to her, but it was no more than the attraction he'd feel for any halfway attractive woman. Maybe he really didn't like some things about her. Maybe he thought she was a bad risk, foolish with her money, lax with her child. Maybe he figured Dennis had had a valid reason for dumping her, like she wasn't any good in bed. God, how long had it been since she'd felt like that?

"Whatever you say."

Grimly, Sam walked over to the girls. He kissed the twins and ruffled Tyree's hair. "Behave yourselves," he ordered. "I'll be back in a couple of hours."

"Thanks, Sam," Tyree said softly.

Sam's mouth twisted into a smile. "You're welcome, cupcake."

Tyree giggled and lightly poked Kim in the ribs. "That's funny. All his special names are sweet stuff. He calls you sugar."

"And Keli's sweetie," Kim said.

"And you're cupcake!" Keli chortled, pointing at Tyree.

"So I like my desserts," Sam teased. "Maybe I have a sweet tooth."

"So what's Mommy?" Tyree asked, laughing.

"Honey!" Kim suggested.

"No, no, candy!" Keli said, and all three girls broke into raucous laughter.

Sierra caught her breath. Sam shot her a look, and the horror in it, the embarrassment, nearly felled her. Switching her gaze away, she stammered about the silliness of little girls, while Sam muttered that he'd better go and did.

Sierra immediately got up to switch on the television and put in the DVD. She took a place on the couch while the girls settled down with pillows on the floor. She meant to watch the movie. She'd enjoyed it the first time, after all, but she knew within minutes that she wouldn't be able to keep her mind on it now. She kept wondering what was wrong with her to put that look in Sam's eyes.

Sam didn't breathe easily until he was home, but even then he didn't fully relax. He kept thinking how awful it would've been if Sierra had come here. As he walked through the small, drab kitchen of the small, drab house, he felt again the overwhelming lack of equality in their standards of living.

He wasn't envious of what Sierra had or ashamed of the way he and the twins lived. Their house, which had been built in the late '50s, was small and tired and colorless, but it was clean and sound and comfortable enough. Cool in the summer, warm in the winter. One day he hoped to provide better. In the meantime the twins had all the advantages to be found at Lana's and Sierra's.

All in all, they had a good life. But if Sierra were to see this house, she'd know without a doubt how far below her he stood on the economic ladder. He wanted—needed—to feel that they were equals, but it wasn't true in any way except one. Business.

That was all he had with Sierra. That was all he could have with Sierra, all his pride and their circumstances would allow. For everyone's sake, he had to protect that. More than once, though, he'd have given almost anything to change the situation. Tonight, for instance, while playing around with that stupid sink sprayer, he'd felt…at home, like he was in the right place, exactly where he and the twins were supposed to be, and then Sierra had gotten into the act, and for a moment that feeling had intensified. He'd had her there in his arms, laughing and tussling, and a feeling that he was afraid even now to analyze had blindsided him, a feeling of such possessiveness, such… He shook his head, unable and unwilling to put a name to it. For an instant, just a heartbeat, he'd have traded his soul to be able to put his mouth to hers, to feel her slide her arms around his neck, and she knew it. Despite everything, she knew that he wanted her. Everyone knew it, even the girls on some level.

"What's Mommy?"

"Honey!"

"Candy!"

Sweet enough to eat with a spoon, that's what "Mommy" was.

Swallowing hard, he headed for the shower, so tired that his feet felt like lead weights. Maybe cold water would invigorate him, clear his head, drum some sense into him. He sighed because he knew he had to go back to Sierra's tonight. And tomorrow. And Monday. And nearly every day after that so long as they were partners. He sighed again because Sierra's was exactly where he wanted to be.

God help him.

Because he wasn't sure how much longer he could help himself.

Chapter Seven

Sam returned long before the movie was over. Sierra had forgotten that it was over three hours in length and so hadn't warned him. The girls were rapt when Sam walked in, barely even sparing him a glance. Sierra, however, could barely tear her gaze away. No one should look that good in jeans, boots and a simple T-shirt.

He dropped down onto the end of the sofa opposite her. It was, unfortunately, a long couch, but a very comfortable one. She curled her legs beneath her and smiled. He glanced irritably at his wristwatch, holding his arm beneath the dim glow of the single lamp that she'd left burning on the tall table behind the sofa.

"How much longer?"

She couldn't give him an exact answer. "I'm not sure what time we started, frankly, but it's pretty long."

He made a face, flattening his lips in unhappy resignation, and settled in to wait. Within minutes she realized that he had fallen asleep, his head dropping onto his own shoulder as his lean frame sprawled against the corner of the sofa. Poor man, he was obviously exhausted.

He worked too hard, but what he had accomplished in the past weeks was nothing short of amazing. One of the greenhouses was finished; seedlings were sprouting in layered rows inside. A ton of fertilizer had been worked into the fields behind the house, and much of the perimeter of the tilled ground had already been planted in rye and wheat, with more to be sowed in the fallow fields and later plowed under again, building nutrients into the soil. Soon Sam would begin stringing wire and build a sturdy trellis row for the rosebushes he'd set out. Last of all, he would sow lavender on the hillside. He had taken care of so much already. It was time someone took care of him.

Sierra tucked her hands between her knees and quelled the urge to touch that almost perfect circle of hair in the center of his hairline. These Jayces were prone to cowlicks, it seemed. She thought it terribly charming.

By the time the movie finally ended, the girls were all fading, but while Keli collapsed facedown on her pillow, Kim rolled over, sat up, glanced at Sam and said softly to Sierra, "That was great!"

"I'm glad you enjoyed it," Sierra whispered.

"Sammy's sleeping," Tyree said around a yawn.

She looked at Kim and asked, "What should we do? I hate to wake him."

Keli sat up then. "I'm too tired to go home," she said plaintively.

"Can't they stay?" Tyree pleaded. "Sam can sleep on the couch."

Sierra considered. If Sam could sleep this deeply sitting up, he didn't have any business driving home. "Okay. Let's get you all upstairs and into bed," she decided.

A soft chorus of cheers applauded her decision. She reached for the remote and shut off the television, then rose and followed the girls from the room. They wandered from the den and down the hall past the never-used formal living room to the stairs, their footsteps dragging sleepily. Sierra literally pushed them up the stairs, hands moving from back to back.

At the top of the stairs, Tyree paused to ask, "Can we sleep in your room? We won't all fit in mine."

She had a point. The girls would want to sleep together. The guest room wasn't furnished to accommodate three sleepers. Sierra's room, on the other hand, featured an enormous king-sized bed ample enough for three little girls.

"Sure, baby."

"Thanks, Mom."

The girls trooped into her room, yawning. Sierra rushed them through brushing their teeth and washing up, then bundled them into sleepwear, tucked them into her own big bed and dispensed kisses.

"Where will you sleep, Mom?" Tyree wanted to know.

"In the guest room, I suppose. Don't worry about me. Just go straight to sleep, because if I know Sam, he'll be out of here at the crack of dawn."

"Oh, yeah," Kim agreed, from the center of the bed between Tyree and Keli.

"Sleep well." They looked like three cuddly kittens tucked up in a basket. Sierra switched off the bedside lamp, then snagged her nightgown and robe from a hook on the bedroom door.

In the nearest guest room she stripped and donned the loose cotton gown. In the act of folding down the bedcovers, she paused and straightened. She couldn't help thinking of Sam sleeping sitting up down there on the sofa. He couldn't rest well in that condition, and he was bound to wake with a terrible crick in his neck. After quickly donning her robe, she pulled a pillow off the bed, picked up a chenille throw from the armchair in the corner and went down to the den.

He had sprawled out a little, one leg flung wide, but otherwise hadn't moved. She looked at her lovely new sofa and his feet and knew that the boots had to be her first order of business. Leaving the pillow and blanket on the coffee table, she crouched down in front of him and lifted his heavy foot. He just bent his knee and moved it away from her, sliding a little farther down into the corner of the cushions. She dusted her hands together, determined that those gritty boots come off.

She moved closer to the couch and bent over, saying softly, "Sam, your boots. Can you help me get them off?"

He huffed a deep breath and muttered something that sounded like, "Shing swart."

She didn't even try to figure that out, just backed up, bent from the waist, picked up his foot and pulled. The boot slid off surprisingly easily. He pulled his leg back and dropped it to the floor. She followed the same procedure with the other foot, and suddenly he sat up straight. She quickly placed the pillow onto the seat cushion next to the arm of the couch. Then she stepped back.

"Stretch out now."

He just blinked at her, looking dazed. Lightly pushing against his shoulders, she repeated her instructions, and he began drifting downward onto his side. She bent and gathered his legs together, lifting them so that he rolled onto his back as he went down. She smiled as she spread the chenille throw over him. Then, on impulse, she bent low and placed a featherlight kiss on the corner of his mouth. Some men, she mused, reaching across the sofa to flip off the subdued light, looked like little boys when they slept. Sam looked just like what he was, a virile young man who could crack the world open like a nut. Any woman in her right mind would be crazy about him. She sure was.

"I'll leave you to sleep now," she told him softly, wishing that it could be otherwise, but just as she started to rise, his hand shot out from beneath the blanket and clamped onto the top of her leg right below the bend of her thigh.

"No," he said, quite distinctly, and Sierra's heart leaped into her throat.

She sat down next to him, perching on the tiny sliver of cushion left to her. For a long moment, she waited breathlessly for what would happen next. Half a dozen heartbeats later, she began to wonder if he was even awake. "Sam?"

"Hmm?"

"Why don't you want me to go?"

He sighed, richly, deeply, and his hand lifted from her leg. Rising caressingly upward, it skimmed over her belly and breast, brushed against her throat and slid around to the nape of her neck. She couldn't breathe. Her nipples had tightened to painful little points, and her heart was slamming in her ears like a big bass drum.

"You know," he said on a long sigh. "Make love."

Make love! She closed her eyes, thrilled down to her toes. Why shouldn't they make love? She and Sam were a great team. With Sam everything seemed so clear, well, maybe, but even when they argued, Sam could always make his point without killing her sense of self, without making her feel small and devalued. This intense physical attraction was just a part of what was, what could be, between them, but she hadn't dared hope.

Now suddenly the future lay spread out before her like a patchwork quilt. The pattern was too complex to discern clearly at this distance, but it was beautiful; and this was her chance to make it happen.

"Oh, Sam."

She slipped off the loose robe and leaned forward.

He was dreaming. He understood that. Grass waved, tall and green, on one side of him, golden wheat on the other. No, not him. Them. They lay on a hillside, close—so close—blue sky and white clouds overhead, a field of flowers below, every color of the rainbow standing in regimented rows. Sun soaked into their bare skin. He had made love to her there on a hillside that didn't exist, looking down on the farm, their farm. He smiled, feeling his own heartbeat, and knew that he would wake soon. Any moment now... Any moment.

"Sam, your boots. Just let me get your boots off."

"Sure thing, sweetheart." *The boots first, then anything else you want.*

Wait. Hadn't they been naked before? Stupid dream.

"Stretch out now."

He was trying to make sense of that when he felt himself falling in slow motion, and then something floated down on top of him, something he couldn't see. He felt a flutter against his cheek and the corner of his mouth. A lovely, flowery scent wafted over him. He knew that scent. Sierra. Suddenly aware of the great heaviness in his groin, he strained upward

toward her, and when he opened his eyes, Sierra
was bending over him. Lovely Sierra. Beautiful Sierra. Sexy, delicious Sierra. He wished he wasn't
so tired, that he could fill his hands with her bright
hair.

"I'll leave you to sleep now."

Leave? She wasn't supposed to leave. She always stayed in his dreams, and they made love,
over and over again. In his dreams.

"No." He shoved at the thing enveloping him
and reached out for her. There. Warm, silky flesh.

"Sam?"

Ah. That was better. His arms felt lighter. The
cobwebs were gone. The ache in his groin intensified.

"Why don't you want me to go?"

Silly question. "You know." He reached up,
found smooth skin, soft hair. Sierra. His Sierra.
How he needed her. Strength and exultation filled
him. He could have what he wanted, everything he
wanted. Sierra. "Make love."

"Oh, Sam."

She was on top of him. Interesting. That's not
how it usually happened. Was that her breast in his
hand? He felt her mouth on his. God, that was
sweet. Better than he remembered. Better than he
usually dreamed. And not quite as good in other
ways. He ached, and he needed to feel pressure on
that ache. If he could get her between his legs, he
could bring her weight more firmly into contact
where he most wanted it, but the right leg felt
trapped, and when he moved the left it fell down

or off.... Where were they? What kind of dream was this? Or was it a dream at all?

He caught her hair in his hands. Soft. Incredibly soft, but alive, satin coiling between his fingers. Her kiss grew a little frantic, and white-hot pleasure slammed through him. Power surged throughout his body, and he poured it into the kiss, eagerly pulling every taste from her, plunging deeper and deeper, searching for her very essence.

He shifted slightly, wanting her beneath him, and he knew then that they were reclining on a couch and that this was no dream. He abruptly sat up. Gasping for air and still disoriented, he glanced around, making out certain shapes in the darkness. There was a lamp, table, chair and moonlight reflecting on a television screen. This was Sierra's den.

He looked at her, stunned that he was awake and here with her. He took in the long fall of her hair, frothing about her shoulders in wild tumbles, and the slow, sultry smile that gleamed pearly in the moonlight. He fuzzily remembered driving back to her house and dropping down onto her couch, irritated that the movie hadn't yet played out. The next thing he knew they were on that hillside, naked. Obviously he'd fallen asleep. The ache in his groin told him that the dream had left him unfulfilled.

His eyes popped wide as she reached down, grasped the hem of her nightgown and peeled it up and off over her head, letting it drop from her fingertips. Before he could stop them, his hands reached out for her. Silk. Warm silk. And so beautiful that she was almost painful to look at, her pale, graceful body gently curving and swelling in all the right places. He knew the many reasons why he shouldn't be here like this with her, but in that moment they just didn't matter.

She lifted onto her knees beside him, and he instinctively rose to meet her, awed by the sylphlike delicacy of her body. Leaning into him, she slid her arms about his neck, bowed her head and lowered her mouth to his. His heart beating with the force of a ball-peen hammer slamming down onto an anvil, he embraced her. They fit together perfectly. He marveled at the match as her mouth plied his.

A familiar surge of masculine energy lifted him, and with it came the urge, the need to possess. Capturing her face in his hands, he pushed her down on her heel, bending her head back with the force of his ravenous mouth. Her hands slid down his body and she tugged urgently at his shirt. He covered one breast with his hand, squeezed it gently, and suddenly she shifted and went down onto her back.

Kneeling between her legs, he looked down at her there, her pale body open to him, hair spread like flame against the dark cushions. Moonlight slanted across her face, showing him the wildness in her eyes, the surrender. He ripped off his shirt and opened his jeans, feeling strong, free, primitive.

She moaned softly, and blind lust swirled together with the frantic need to please her. He twisted around, thrust his legs out in front of him, shucked his jeans, his shorts, his socks in one long, smooth motion.

"Sam," she said, reaching for him.

He moved into her arms and stretched out atop her. Their mouths melded in the sweetest kiss imaginable. He let his trembling hands wander, caress, probe, until—both frantic now—he joined their bodies. She put her head back and made a sound somewhere between laughter and sobbing.

"Sierra?" he asked uncertainly.

"Yes," she whispered. "Oh, yes."

He lifted himself above her and began stroking them both toward oblivion.

She gripped the soft, knit blanket beneath her with both hands, placed her feet flat against the cushions and curled her spine upward. Nothing in her experience had prepared her for the wonder of being loved by Sam Jayce. Nothing could have. Such tenderness, such power was unimaginable. She had known that he was young and strong and handsome, but she hadn't realized that he was physically, sexually perfect, filling every part of her with an authority that frankly astounded.

He didn't try to kiss her again, just held himself there above her and systematically turned her mind to jelly with the full, rhythmic stroke of his body against and into hers. She couldn't even give back, only take, exult in and survive the taking. She made sounds, wordless exclamations of wonder completely beyond her control.

At one point she managed to reach up and splay

her hands against the sides of his head. He turned
his face into one palm, sank his teeth into the tender
flesh of her wrist and never faltered in his rhythm.
Her head spun, and blackness broke over her. She
cried out, and he gave her his weight then, his
mouth coming down over hers, his tongue driving
into the sound that flowed up out of her throat.

Sometime afterward she floated up from the
abyss and into swelling awareness. He slid down
her body and found her breasts with his mouth and
hands. Within moments she was gasping and buck-
ing beneath him again. Rising above her once more,
he began stroking slow and deep, filling her utterly
again and again.

He carried her higher this time, to the very stars,
the rush of sensation frightening in its intensity,
glorious in its completion. She screamed. She cried.
Or did she? Perhaps. She didn't know. Floating in
a sea of euphoria with Sam as her anchor, her sanc-
tuary, she didn't care.

Gradually, she realized that it was Sam who
churned that sea into tumult, who drove the waves
upon which she rode, reaching for his own completion, and that he had never ceased. Gladly, she
wrapped her arms and legs around him and held
him as he stroked closer and closer to his destina-
tion. She held him tighter as he began to shudder,
as his muscles grew rigid and his head drew back,
jaws clamping against a roar he would not let out.
She held him until his flesh melted into pliability
and his head fell forward onto her shoulder and,

finally, his bulk settled onto her in boneless collapse.

She felt the spurting heat deep inside, and closed her eyes, happy, even with the knowledge that they had been inexcusably foolish on at least one level. Perhaps love was always foolish. She only knew that nothing and no one could ever equal Sam. Lifting his head with her hands, she brought her mouth to his, kissing him with all the grateful wonder in her. Love like this was worth any foolishness, any risk, any effort.

"Sam. Sam. Sam." She kissed his name onto his lips, again and again, never suspecting that he could simply sit up and leave her until, suddenly, he was doing just that. "Where are you going?"

"Home." He snatched up his underwear, stuck his legs through and pulled it up. "Where I'm supposed to be." He reached for his jeans. "Where are the girls?"

"A-asleep upstairs."

He yanked his socks on. "I'll be back for them in the morning."

"Sam, please, you can't just go."

"Can't? Can't?" he parroted angrily. "*This* is what I can't do, Sierra, what I've already done!" He stomped his feet into his boots.

"Why?"

Snatching up her gown, he shot to his feet and threw it at her. "This is not a love affair, it's a business arrangement!"

She sat up, crossing her legs and shielding her

body with the nightgown. "This has *nothing* to do with business."

He found his shirt, tossed it on over his head. "We can't pretend the business doesn't exist, Sierra."

"I'm not saying we should."

"We're risking everything, the whole future of the operation," he argued, stabbing first one arm and then the other through the shirtsleeves.

"I don't see how."

He rounded on her, shouting though he kept his volume tightly leashed. "I'll tell you how. We're mismatched, Sierra. Our circumstances are just too different. I could never compare with you, not as an equal. It's stupid to think otherwise."

"That's absurd."

"No. That's fact. You want it in numbers? You want it in black and white? Ask your attorney. Ask the accountants. Ask anyone!"

"I don't care what anyone else says about it!"

"No? I do. I've worked too hard to be someone I can be proud of, someone the girls can be proud of. I can't let anything get in the way of that. I just can't. They already have too many strikes against them. I won't have it said that their brother's no better than a gold-digging gigolo."

"Oh, Sam, no. Don't even think such a thing. I never would. I never could."

"It's what they would all say, the whole town." He sounded tired, sad. "You know it is."

"Not if the farm is a success."

"Well, it isn't a success. Not yet, and maybe

never, especially if we keep doing this.'' He strode toward the door.

''Sammy, please, don't leave.''

He paused, and she reached out to him there in the shadows with every ounce of emotion in her. ''I don't have a choice,'' he finally said in a choked voice. ''I never did.''

Sierra collapsed back onto the sofa, listening to his footsteps clap hollowly through the house. Her body still hummed with the magic he had worked in her, but her heart felt as if a fist had reached into her chest and squeezed it dry. She wept for a long while, silent tears gliding from her eyes and past her ears to wet her hair.

How stupid could she be, seducing him like that when he was half-asleep? How could she have forgotten how proud he was? How dedicated? He was only trying to do the best for everyone. She understood. She could see the situation from his eyes, but that wasn't the only way to see it.

He didn't realize how lucky they were. Maybe his youth played against him in that, but she knew how rare this thing between them was. Well, maybe he didn't know, but he wasn't stupid. He would see. He would learn. He had to.

Sitting up, she fumbled with the nightgown until she found the front and pulled it on. Then she shifted to the other end of the couch, laid her head on the pillow against which he had so briefly rested and slipped beneath the chenille cover. She would sleep here where they had made love and try to believe that he would come to his senses.

Chapter Eight

"Morning, Sam."

He was later than she had expected and obviously wary, but she didn't let that deter her. Rising from the table, she moved across the kitchen and greeted him with a casual kiss on the cheek. The girls, watching from the breakfast nook, giggled. Sam glowered and cleared his throat. His arms were full of fresh changes of clothing for the twins. He shifted his gaze over her shoulder, addressing the girls.

"Morning. How was the movie?"

"Great!"

As the twins launched into a vivid, disjointed description of the cinematic treat, Sierra calmly turned away and took an extra plate from the warming oven, while Sam moved toward the table. He draped a change of clothing over the backs of each of the twins' chairs, nodding and murmuring assent as they unfolded the story. Sierra carried the plate to the table and set it down next to her own.

"I hope you like waffles," she said when the discourse died down. "The girls insisted on having them this morning." She ignored the refusal in his eyes.

"They're yummy," Keli announced.

"And they're already made," Sierra added, forking two large, buttered waffles onto the heated plate, "so you might as well sit down and eat." She smiled and reached for a bowl of strawberries. "Fruit?"

His gaze met hers, telegraphing his feelings perfectly. He didn't like acting as though last night hadn't happened, but he didn't have a choice in front of the girls. She spooned the fruit onto the waffles and reached for the syrup.

He stepped over the chair and sat down, mumbling, "Looks good."

She tried not to smirk. "We only have maple. Hope that's okay."

"Sure."

Sierra poured maple syrup onto his plate until he lifted a hand to stop her. After a moment's hesitation, he picked up his knife and fork and cut into the waffles. Though clean-shaven and ready for work, he looked rough around the edges. She hadn't got much rest herself, and she wasn't above hoping that it had been the same for him, so just as he delivered the first bite to his mouth, she asked, "Sleep well?"

He cut her a sideway glance that could have drawn blood, before dropping his gaze to his plate and beginning to eat with single-minded efficiency.

The girls finished one by one and left to dress for the day. The twins had their outing with Lana, and Tyree's father was coming for her, having planned a weekend with his elderly parents in Houston. Since they were meeting at the shop, Sierra had already packed Tyree's bag. Keli was the last to leave the room. As soon as she was out of earshot, Sam laid down his fork and looked at Sierra.

"Sierra, about last night—"

"Last night was wonderful," she said, stabbing a piece of waffle with her fork, "right up until the moment you decided it shouldn't be." She poked the bite of waffle into her mouth and chewed.

He pinched the bridge of his nose. "I didn't decide any such thing."

She swallowed. "Really? That's what it sounded like to me."

"All I said was that it shouldn't have happened."

"And I disagree," she informed him.

"Damn it, Sierra," he hissed, "I won't—"

"Sam?"

Clamping his jaw shut, he whipped his head around. Kim and Tyree stood side by side in the doorway. Kim was holding one of Tyree's shirts in front of her.

"Can I wear this today? Please?"

Sam rubbed the back of his neck wearily. "I don't see why that's necessary."

"But it's so much prettier than mine," Kim said, adding with a gush of praise, "Tyree has the coolest clothes."

Sierra groaned inwardly.

"Your clothes are the best I can afford, Kim," Sam snapped.

Kim seemed shocked. "I—I know. I just like Tyree's top better."

"Your things were always good enough before."

Kim blinked and Tyree sent a puzzled glance at her mother. Sierra gently laid a hand on Sam's forearm. He snatched away, then glanced worriedly at the girls and drew a deep, calming breath.

"Your clothes are very pretty, Kim," Sierra said calmly, "and you're so very pretty yourself that it wouldn't matter if they weren't."

"Yeah," Tyree said helpfully. "Your top's a lot better than that one, and besides, you're littler than me. This one probably wouldn't even fit."

Kim gazed uncertainly at Sam. "Yeah. Probably. I'll just wear mine then." She gave the shirt back to Tyree with a bright smile for Sam.

Sam abruptly rose from the table and strode from the room, muttering, "I'll start the truck. Lana's waiting."

Kim shot a look at Sierra, saying in a small voice, "Better hurry, I guess."

"You go ahead," Sierra told her gently. "Tyree and I will clean up here."

Kim nodded and hurried away, head down.

"What's the matter with Sam?" Tyree wanted to know, coming to stand next to her mother.

Sierra brushed a lock of hair from her daughter's shoulder. "I think he's embarrassed that he can't buy the nice things for Kim and Keli that I buy for you."

Tyree frowned thoughtfully. "Yeah. Dad says that, too. He says it's not fair that you can have all the money and he can't have any of it."

"He's wrong, baby," Sierra told her gently. "It's not fair or unfair. It just is. They're both wrong, Dennis and Sam, because money isn't what matters. It's the kind of people we are that matters most, and Sam is one of the very best people I've ever known."

"Kim and Keli, too," Tyree said matter-of-factly.

"Yes."

Tyree bit her lip. "Mom, do you think Sam's a better dad than Dad? I mean, he's more like their dad than their brother."

Sierra felt a brief impulse to enumerate all of Dennis Carlton's many faults as a parent and a human being, but she didn't follow it. Instead, she drew her daughter onto her knee and said, "I don't think I'm a good judge of that, Tyree, and I don't really think it matters. Dennis is your dad, good, bad or indifferent, and you love him. That's all that counts as far as I'm concerned."

Tyree nodded, a small smile gently lifting the corners of her mouth. "Thanks, Mom," she said, sounding very adult. Sierra hugged her tightly for a moment.

"I just want you to be happy, and I understand that your father is part of that. Now let's get this table cleared. Okay?"

They both stood and began clearing the table.

"Mom?" Tyree asked after a moment. "Is Sam your boyfriend?"

Sierra froze, her hands laden with dirty, sticky dishes. "Sam's my p-partner."

"But you like him."

"Well, yes, but I don't think...that is, Sam doesn't... Actually, I like Sam a whole lot, and I think we'd be good together, but we're a long way from making any kind of commitment. Do you understand what I mean?"

Tyree shrugged. "Yeah, I guess. I hope you get married, though. That way the twins would be like my sisters."

Sierra couldn't seem to get her breath. "You hope Sam and I get married?"

"Sure," Tyree said, flashing a smile. "If you want to, I mean."

Sierra wrapped her arms around her daughter "You know what, I just might. But I don't think Sam's ready to think about that yet, so it's best that we keep any talk of marriage to ourselves."

"I won't say anything," Tyree promised.

"Good. I don't think Sam would like it if you mentioned it to the twins."

Tyree nodded. "Okay."

She began gathering dirty dishes and after a moment moved off into the kitchen. Sierra sat down, a little weak in the knees. Even her little girl could see that she and Sam would be a good match. What, she wondered, would it take for Sam to understand that?

Sam felt as though he was being eaten alive from the inside out. He thought every moment about making love to Sierra, alternately castigating himself for having allowed it to happen and mentally reliving every incredible sensation. He knew that he would remember for the rest of his life what it was like to make love with her.

That was where it had to stop, however, for all their sakes. People would talk if he and Sierra went public with a romantic relationship. Shoot, they were already talking. Sam had heard from Gwyn Dunstan that Heston Searle was going around making cracks about Sierra buying herself a younger man. It would be worse if they went public, and he couldn't subject the twins to that. God knew they'd had enough gossip swirling around them already. Knowing that Tyree would be out of town with her father all weekend, he decided to take the time on Saturday morning to set Sierra straight about their relationship.

He dropped the girls off at Lana and Chet's and headed back out to the farm. When he got there, he went in through the rear door, same as usual, and called Sierra by name. When she didn't answer, he moved to the intercom mounted on the wall beneath a cabinet and studied the buttons. Choosing one which indicated that it would provide sound to the whole house, he spoke into the microphone.

"Sierra? It's Sam. Can we talk?"

Her voice came to him through the speaker. "Sure. Come on up."

"Where are you?"

"The study. Just come up the stairs, second door on the right."

He walked through the house into the rotunda portion of the entry and stood at the foot of the stairs. Making a face, he climbed the steps and warily approached the study. Before he got there, however, Sierra came out onto the landing. Her hair was down, and she wore soft black sweats and a bright smile, feet bare.

"Hi. I'm so glad you're here." She waltzed closer.

"Sierra, I need to talk to you."

"Absolutely. After."

"After what?"

Smiling, she reached down and peeled the sweatshirt up. Sam staggered back. She wasn't wearing a bra. The sweatshirt hit the floor, and before he could get his breath, she'd shoved down the pants and kicked them away, as well. He nearly swallowed his tongue. Sweet merciful heaven, the woman was as naked as the day she was born and so damned fine that he could've cried. She slipped closer, both dangerous and seductive. He couldn't take his eyes off her. Then suddenly she flew to him, throwing her arms around his neck. His own arms, operating independently of his brain, went around her waist, and then they were kissing, devouring one another with lips and teeth and tongues.

His mind was screaming, "Run!" But his body was laughing, "Too late!" And so it was. She urged him backward, walking in his arms, feet shuffling and tangling, bodies bumping with electric results. He realized dimly that she was pulling at his shirt and automatically lifted his arms, trying to maintain the contact between their mouths. When she broke it, ripping his shirt off over his head, he felt such intense irritation that he grabbed her about the waist and hauled her right back again. Their naked skin made breathtaking contact, and he knew that if he couldn't get inside her at once he was going to explode into bits.

He scooped her off her feet. She pointed to a door, and he carried her through it. It was a large room, done up in yellows and golds, with a splash of hot pink. A white-rock fireplace filled the wall next to the big bed with its heavy, scrolled iron headboard. A matching bench stood beneath one window, and a comfortable armchair sat before another. A large dresser shared another wall with a door that opened into a large bath.

The bed was unmade, the covers rumpled and bunched as if she'd just crawled from beneath them. Somehow, that only added to the dark desire pulsing through his veins. He dropped her on the bed and watched her pose herself for maximum effect while he stripped off the rest of his clothes. She need not have bothered; he was beyond control at that point. In point of fact, he fell on her like a ravening beast, no finesse, no patient stimulation or romantic caresses, just pure, blazing lust. If this was what she wanted, he told himself savagely, this was what she would get, but just this. *Just* this.

Punitive in his attentions, he drove her straight to the edge and kept her there, prolonging the moment of release until she begged him, twisting and mewling, clutching and even pummeling his back with her fists, but he held her off as long as he could, just because he could and because it was such devastatingly sweet torture. In the end, they went over together, with the husky cries of animals. Shaken by the magnitude of it, he found himself on his back sometime later, with Sierra beside him, panting softly.

Damnation, why did it have to be so good? Why did something so wrong for both of them have to feel so blasted right? It made him helpless to resist what she offered so freely, and that demanded a certain ruthlessness on his part, which wasn't how he wanted to play this at all. She just didn't leave him any options. So be it, then. He rolled up onto his shoulder and looked down at her. The woman was sex personified—blatantly female, boldly arousing and downright greedy in it.

"This doesn't change anything," he told her. "That's what you have to understand. On the one hand we have the business, just as we laid it out. On the other hand, we have *this*." For emphasis, he palmed her breast, fingers plucking the neat, coral nipple. "Sex. That's all it is. That's all it can ever be."

"Because people will talk," she said breathlessly.

"That's part of it, yes."

"Because, according to you, we're not equals outside of bed and business."

"It's not something I dreamed up, Sierra. There's no question about it. You pushed this, but there's no future in it. Do you understand what I'm saying?"

"I understand what you're saying perfectly," she purred, but the look in her eyes troubled him, until she boldly reached down and took him in hand. He moaned, falling over onto his back. Well, hell, if a man's resolve was going to be beat all to flinders, this was the way to have it done.

She straddled him, and using both hands, had him crazy again in a twinkling.

Just sex, he told himself as madness took hold again. Just the best damned sex imaginable.

Sierra stayed in the bed when Sam finally rose, dressed and left to pick up the twins. He didn't kiss her goodbye, but she didn't expect it. She had proved to him that the attraction between them was too strong to dismiss, but this was a war that one battle could not possibly win, and Sam's position was deeply entrenched.

Flopping onto her back, she stared up at the ceiling. This was either the smartest or the stupidest thing she'd ever done. Physically, she felt so replete that her muscles were almost too relaxed to obey. Emotionally, she felt raw.

She'd had to bite her tongue repeatedly in the past hours to keep from telling him that she loved him, and knowing that he wouldn't want to hear it was tearing her in two. Yet, what else could she do? Allowing him to put distance between them wouldn't get her anywhere. She had no choice but to fight with the weapons at her disposal, and if that meant sex, well, she didn't suppose that she was the first woman ever to think of it. The risk, however, was extreme.

Every time he touched her she loved him a little more and her heart grew a bit more fragile, so if this didn't work, she knew that she would shatter inside. The price of failure was a lifetime without him. It was too late to abandon the fight, however, so all she could do was battle on and hope for the best. She would fight, using her body and everything else at her disposal, and pray that his heart could not hold itself aloof forever.

Sam dropped the hammer he'd been using to tack up plastic water tubing along the framework of the greenhouse above the raised beds and looked at the small rectangular object that Sierra had placed in his hand.

"What the hell is this?"

Sierra answered him in the same disgruntled tone. "You know perfectly well that it's a cell phone."

Frowning, he thrust it at her. "Take it back."

"I can't take it back. I had to sign a contract when I activated it. Besides, I want you to have it."

The frown gave way to ire. "Damn it, Sierra! Do you really think you can buy me with the latest gadgets?"

Her mouth dropped open. "Buy you? What kind of nonsense is that? I'm not trying to buy you. I just thought you could use a cell phone."

"I'm not a high-tech pet. I don't come when I'm called," he retorted smartly.

She bit back a hot reply and put a hand to her head. Trust him to put the one spin on it that would most offend his vaunted pride. She'd assumed that he would grumble, but she couldn't believe that he wouldn't see the wisdom of being in easy contact. She folded her arms and said sarcastically, "You are such a *man.*"

His whole stance changed from one of rigid rejection to one of smug sensual awareness. "I was pretty sure you'd noticed that already."

"It wasn't a compliment," she snapped, fighting the urge to fan herself. The weather outside was cool and cloudy, but inside the greenhouse, the temperature was downright toasty—and getting warmer. They'd need those fans Sam was getting set to install for summer use, just as they needed the cell phones. "Do you know how insulting you're being? Do you really think I'm the sort of woman to buy herself a man? And if I were, isn't a cell phone selling yourself pretty short?"

His lips quirked. "I trust there isn't a double meaning behind that."

"It's not about *us*," she told him, shaking her hands because she couldn't shake him. "It's about you getting ready to tackle that south field."

He looked skeptically at the cell phone in his hand. "What about it?"

"Think, Sam. When Kim fell, the urgent care staff wouldn't touch her until you got there. Lana had to track me down, then I had to track you down. What happens if I'm out of the office next time? Or if I can't find you?"

His brow wrinkled. "People have and do get along just fine without—"

"Right," she interrupted, all too familiar with that argument. "And every day people are maimed, and even die, because they're alone or can't be reached when something awful happens. Everything new isn't necessarily bad, Sam."

He clapped a hand over the nape of his neck, considering the miniature phone in his hand. Finally he asked, "How much?"

"Forty bucks a month. Each. I have one, too." She wouldn't tell him just then that the phones themselves cost a couple hundred bucks apiece. "I think it's a perfectly justifiable business expense."

He lifted an eyebrow. "So the business is paying for it?"

"If you want. I didn't feel I ought to make that decision without consulting you first, but I certainly have no objections."

He frowned, but then he slid the thing into his pocket. She looked down to hide her smile and rocked back on her toes. "When you're ready, I'll show you how to use it. By the way, it clips on your belt, if you want.''

''By the way, I knew that, and I think I can figure out the rest.''

''Fine!'' Throwing up her hands, she whirled and stalked toward the door.

''Hey!''

She stopped and turned, arms swinging out at her sides. ''What?''

He patted the pocket containing the phone. ''Emergencies only. Okay? I don't have time for chitchat.''

''Who does?'' She was halfway around when he stopped her again.

''Wait a minute.''

''What is it now?''

He crooked a finger, his pale eyes darkening, and her heart rate sped up. ''Come here.''

She stabbed her hands onto her hips and gave him back his own words. ''I am not a pet that comes when it's called high-tech, low-tech or otherwise.''

He grinned. ''No, what you are is a royal pain in the butt.''

''Well, at least we have that in common,'' she said with sweet sarcasm.

''Maybe. Now if you'll get your sweet butt over here so I can get my hands on it, we'll see what else we might have in common.''

She wanted really badly to turn on her heel and walk out of there, leaving him hanging just this once, but she couldn't do it. The pull of those sage-green eyes and knowingly tilted mouth was just too strong. She waltzed forward, intending to give as good as she got. "Why didn't you say so?"

His grin widened as she came to halt within easy reach. "I just did."

"Your technique could use work."

He laughed and slid his hands across her shoulders to the back of her head. "I didn't hear you complaining about my technique before."

"You are irritatingly smug," she told him, but she couldn't stop the smile that tickled the corner of her mouth. He leaned forward and tickled that same corner with the tip of his tongue, but instead of kissing her, he slid his mouth to her ear.

"Maybe I have reason to be smug."

"I can't imagine what makes you think so," she retorted breathlessly.

He dropped his hands to her bottom and yanked her hard against him, putting himself snugly between her thighs. "Maybe it's the bruises you put on my back."

She gasped. "I didn't! Did I? Oh, Sam! I'm sorry, I didn't realize...." He was showing so much tooth that he was in danger of blinding her with the glare. She narrowed her eyes. "Either you're lying or you're very pleased."

"No and yes." His hands flexed on her bottom. "Sweetheart, I'll take all the bruises you can dish out." His fingers began gathering up the bottom of her black miniskirt, and he ducked his head to nip the flesh of her throat. "In fact, I'll take a few right now if you can get out of those stockings."

Sierra gulped, her eyelids fluttering. She fought to maintain reason. The first two times had been spur-of-the-moment, unplanned. The first was instigated by a sleepy man and a comfortable couch. The second had been pure impulse; he'd dropped the opportunity right in her lap and just at the moment when she'd feared he would succeed at putting distance between them. But she'd promised herself that she wouldn't take any more chances. She sucked air, felt her breasts swell against his chest and made herself say it.

"I don't suppose you have a c-condom?"

He did pretty much what she'd expected, dropped his hands, backed up and looked at her as if she'd just pulled the rug out from under him. "Is that a problem? Because we didn't use one before."

"It's just that I prefer it," she improvised quickly, "e-especially when I'm on my way to work and don't have time to, ah, clean up."

He frowned and adjusted his shoulders. "Guess I'll buy condoms."

"I'd appreciate that." She kissed him quickly. "Later, okay?"

He shrugged indifferently, but he had the look of a man riding the knife-edge of disappointment. She moved toward the door, knowing she had to get out of there before she gave in, not that she liked refusing him. Maybe she'd pick up a few foil packets herself so this wouldn't happen again, because she was determined to do whatever it took to keep Sam from backing off.

That did not include confessing that she hadn't used the Pill in nearly eight long years.

Chapter Nine

Sierra kept her eyes closed as Sam lifted his head, breaking the kiss.

The girls were downstairs doing homework. Tyree was helping the twins with a picture scroll illustrating Native American traditions. It was a project she'd done herself the year before last. Content to let her handle it, Sierra and Sam had climbed the stairs to the study ostensibly to go over this month's expenses. They hadn't wasted much time with that, finding better uses for the desk.

Sam covered the pulse point at the base of her throat with his hand, then dragged it downward until it cupped her breast. She arched her back, encouraging him to get on with undressing her. He'd already opened her jeans, and now his fingers moved to the placket of her blouse. She squirmed to get away from the corner of the desk blotter jabbing her in the rib and reached for his shirttail.

He smiled and lifted her hand to his mouth, sucking her finger inside. Her eyes nearly crossed as she felt the pull all the way down to the apex of her thighs. In moments like these, she knew that Sam was her other half, and she couldn't believe that eventually he wouldn't know it, too. Meanwhile, he was making her crazy. She reached for him again, but he batted her hand away, chuckling.

"In a hurry, are we?"

Capturing both her wrists in one of his, he stretched them over her head, leaning forward as he did so. She caught her breath, lifting her breasts toward his mouth. He licked the path between them revealed by the opening in the front of her shirt, and it was exactly then that the doorknob rattled.

"Mom?" They both turned their heads at the sound of Tyree's voice, momentarily frozen. The doorknob rattled again, and they exploded into action, bolting up from the desk, grabbing at buttons and zippers and misplaced desktop accessories. "Mom, can we have sodas, ple-e-e-ase?"

Sam looked around, as if trying to decide where to place himself. Sierra pushed him toward a chair in front of the desk, one hand smoothing her hair as she lunged for the door. Yanking it open, she tried her best to behave normally.

"Sodas? Well, let's see. You've already had a soda today. How about milk instead, chocolate milk?"

Tyree glanced at the twins for approval and received eager nods. Kim stuck her head inside the room and addressed Sam, who sat forward in the chair, watching over his shoulder. "Can we, Sam? Can we have chocolate milk?"

He cleared his throat. "How's the project coming?"

"Good. Tyree showed us how to outline everything in black marker so it's real neat."

"Except the buffalo looks kind of like a lion," Keli said, wrinkling her nose.

Sam smiled. "I'm sure it's fine."

"How come the door was locked?" Tyree asked abruptly.

Sierra stifled a gulp and shrugged. "I must've done it accidentally."

"Oh. So should I use the syrup or that powder stuff?"

"The powder has vitamins," Sierra said, glancing at Sam. "Why don't you use that?"

"Okay. Thanks, Mom."

"Thanks, Sam," the twins added.

"No problem. Just be careful not to make a mess."

"We will."

"And drink quick, we'll be going in a few minutes."

"So soon?" Tyree whined.

Sam brushed Sierra with a slightly accusing gaze, saying, "Your mom and I are almost finished here. It's getting late."

The twins hurried for the stairs, Tyree following with reluctant acceptance. Sierra closed the door.

"Do you really have to go so soon?"

His eyes raked her. "We can't keep taking chances like this, Sierra."

Panic, tinged with unreasonable anger, shook her. They had already taken chances, very big chances. Why stop now? But she couldn't say that to Sam.

She lifted her chin and said, much more calmly than she felt, "Then we'll just have to be more careful." He stared at her for a long while, and she dared not breathe until he nodded curtly and looked away. "I'd better go help the girls," she murmured, knowing that it was unwise to press him further at that moment.

She swept from the room, disappointed that they had been interrupted, not that she believed quick sex was going to convince Sam that they belonged together. If that were so, he'd already be convinced. It was the only way she had, though, of maintaining the intimacy, the connection, and she wanted Sam so badly that she was willing to take him any way she could get him, any way at all.

Sam lightly closed the master bedroom door, Sierra beside him, and headed for the stairs, as eager as an inexperienced boy with his first girl. The condoms were burning a hole in his pocket, and the self-disgust that underlay the lust was not enough to send him home without indulging his body in Sierra's. It didn't seem to make any difference how often they "indulged," and it *was* often, he just kept coming back for more. Even nearly getting caught by the girls that night in Sierra's study hadn't appreciably slowed them down, and still he was so wound up and ready for her that when Sierra caught his arm just as he was about to descend the stairs, he glanced back at her irritably.

She gave her head a little jerk. "Let's go to the guest room."

"We can't do that!" he insisted, dropping his voice to a hiss. "We can't have sex with the girls sleeping just down the landing."

"At least the guest room has a lock on the door," Sierra hissed back at him. "The den doesn't have a door at all! What if one of the girls gets up and comes downstairs? What then?"

Sam clapped a hand to the back of his neck. "I should just go home."

"Don't," she said, pulling at him. "I want to make love with you on a real bed for a change."

Sam had to admit that a real bed did sound inviting. That couch downstairs was narrow and confining, and while taking her up against a wall or over a desk was exciting in the extreme, he had the bruises to prove that easier ways definitely existed. He glanced warily at the master bedroom door, behind which all three girls were bedded down for the night, and conceded with a nod.

Smiling triumphantly, Sierra caught him by the hand and literally danced at the end of his arm until he followed her with growing enthusiasm toward the guest room, ignoring the niggling certainty that he was the one doing the dancing and it was almost always to her tune. No matter how convincingly he told himself that he had the upper hand in this, he very much feared that he did not. Yet when she opened her arms to him, he followed her down onto that bed and didn't rise again until nearly two hours later.

As he reached for his jeans, she reached for him, sitting up and pressing herself against his back, arms encircling his neck. She nipped at his shoulder with her perfect little teeth and whispered hopefully into his ear, "Stay with me, Sam. Don't go home tonight."

He wanted to stay. He wanted to make love to her, then sleep with her in his arms, and that more than anything else drove him toward the door. "I can't do that. I won't have the girls find me here in the morning."

"Would it be so bad, Sam?" she asked softly. "If they knew we were together as a couple?"

He wanted to shout at her then, wanted to yell that they were not a couple, but he was too honest to say it, just because it should be so. Instead, he hung his head, warring with the various parts of himself. He felt pulled into pieces at times, wanting different things; the parts that most wanted Sierra usually won, and more and more of him seemed to be falling into that category the longer this went on. That was another reason he had to go.

"I'll see you tomorrow," he said, pulling on his jeans and trying not to feel guilty at the look of disappointment on her face. He stomped his feet into his boots, grabbed his shirt, kissed her quickly and got out of there, but he wasn't any happier about it than she was.

He wasn't happy about much of anything these days. He wasn't happy that he couldn't seem to turn down what she consistently offered or that his work was suffering because of it, and he wasn't happy that leaving her just got more and more difficult. Yet he just couldn't convince himself to end it. He felt trapped by the taste of heaven in a hell of his own making, and he didn't have the slightest idea what he was going to do about it.

He had decided to plant wheat. A farm was a farm, after all, and it just wasn't possible to put all their arable acreage into flowers, which were labor intensive. The wheat would require little enough from him until harvest, and if he found that he couldn't manage both crops, he could always plow under the mature plants and increase the nutritional value of the soil. Besides, he'd cut his farming teeth on wheat. He liked the idea of having a standing field, and he'd have it in the ground in plenty of time to start the other planting, which could only come after the last hard freeze, early March in his estimation. Only one thing was for sure about winter in Texas, though—or any season, for that matter—it simply couldn't be reliably predicted. No more than Sierra Carlton could be.

Now there was a correlation—Sierra Carlton and Texas. Both could be hotter than a pistol, even in the middle of winter. A fellow just couldn't say what he'd find in either case when he opened up for business of a morning. They were both beautiful, wild at heart and utterly compelling.

As if to confirm that thought, something caught Sam's attention, a flash in the corner of his eye. Turning his head, he found the movement and made out the shape. Bringing the tractor to a halt in the center of the field, he sat there, staring out of the glass-enclosed cab at the luxury sedan laying down a trail of dust that led straight to him. It was Sierra. He touched the mobile phone clipped to his belt. If an emergency had cropped up, she'd have called. That left certain scintillating possibilities. Jeez Louise, what wouldn't that woman do?

The answer to that increased the temperature inside the tractor cab to uncomfortable levels. He kept telling himself that he wasn't going to dance to her tune, but damn if his feet didn't take off after other parts of his body just as soon as she started piping her siren's song. He could no longer sell himself the lie that it was just sex, either, because if that was the case, the novelty would surely have worn off by now. One of them would have lost interest. Instead, he practically panted every time she looked his way, and the fact of the matter was, those feelings were getting stronger, not weaker, with time.

Now here she came in the middle of the day, way out in the back of nowhere, and he couldn't quell the rising desire. He glanced around. They were as alone as they could get out here, so why not? But, by golly, if he was going to dance to her tune again, he was damned sure going to lead. Shutting off the engine, he starting climbing down out of the cab.

By the time he reached the ground and headed for the road, she was standing beside her car with the handle of a picnic hamper clutched in both hands.

"Lunchtime," she called cheerily, and so it was, but lunch could wait.

Shrugging out of his denim jacket, he tossed it over one shoulder. She smiled, looking perfectly edible in flowing, deep olive-green, wide-legged pants and a matching sweater with a wide, ribbed collar that hugged her shoulders, baring their tops. A chill breeze ruffled her long, wild hair, but the sunshine, a little shelter and body heat—lots of body heat—would keep them comfortable. He leaped across the narrow ditch running alongside the dirt road and dropped his jacket on the hood of her car, grabbed the picnic basket from her and snagged her hand without breaking stride. She whipped around in his wake and hurried to keep up.

"Where are we going?"

He hauled her around the end of her car. "Not far."

Setting the picnic basket in the bed of the dually, he yanked open the back door and picked her up by the waist, depositing her on the edge of the seat.

"What are you doing?"

"Getting comfortable." He yanked off his cap and sailed it through the door before reaching back over his shoulder, grasping a handful of T-shirt and pulling it up and off. "My back seat's bigger than yours." He wadded the shirt into his hands and shot it through the open door like a basketball. She opened her mouth, only to yelp when he reached for her feet. "Don't need these." He tossed her shoes over the front seat and lifted his hands to her waist, curling his fingers into the elastic waistband of her pants. "Don't need these, either."

Her hands suddenly clamped down over his. "D-don't you even want to know why I'm here?" she asked breathlessly.

"Not particularly," he admitted, "so long as there's sex involved."

She recoiled as if he'd punched her, and he instantly regretted the hasty words. This situation was as much his doing as hers, after all. The impulse to take out on her his shame at his own willingness to compromise his better judgment was both unfair and dishonorable. She deserved better. That was a whole lot of the problem. He set about repairing the damage.

"I didn't mean that the way it sounded. It's just that you're positively addictive. I tell myself I can walk away from this at any time, but the fact is that when you're within reach, I ache to get my hands on you, and when you're not, I can't help wondering when you will be again."

"Sam," she said, sliding her hands into his hair, "I feel the same way about you. I think about you all the time."

He closed his eyes. "I wish you didn't. If just one of us could put a stop to this, we'd both be better off."

"That's not so!" she said in a rush. "Don't you understand yet that I lo—"

He shook her, shook that word right out of her mouth before she could say it. This was his greatest fear. The forever kind of love that Sierra deserved just wasn't in the cards for the two of them. "Sierra, why can't you see that we're headed for a fall, and a big one at that?"

"No! It doesn't have to be that way. We're so good together, Sam."

"We are so headed for trouble," he countered. "Listen, I know what I'm talking about. My folks started out just like this, Sierra. You wouldn't have known it to look at my mom after a few years with Jonah, but she was from a wealthy family in Denver, and my father, well, he just wasn't in the same class. Okay? She thought they could make it. She chose him, and after they wrote her off and he realized he could never give her a life anywhere close to what she was used to, it—it just set up the whole cycle of abuse that finally destroyed them both."

"You're not like Jonah," she insisted sternly.

"No, no, I'm not, and I don't want to be, but I know me, Sierra. I saw the festering resentment in my parents' marriage, and I'm not willing to set myself up for that by sacrificing my pride, especially since pride's about all I've got."

"But why does it have to be that way, just because I unexpectedly inherited some money?"

"No, not just because of that. Don't you think I know who your father is? He's some big shot new-car dealer with businesses all over Fort Worth."

"And he practically cut me off when I married Dennis."

"Your marriage to Dennis is a case in point, Sierra. From what you say, money destroyed it."

She put her hands to her head. "The *lack* of money. But that can't happen again. I'm the one with the money now, and nobody can take it away from me."

"And nobody should," Sam said. "That's the point, Sierra. Letting you invest your money in me and taking it as my own are two different things."

"But you wouldn't be!"

"Which only means that we'd remain unequal, and I'm telling you flatly that I can't live with that."

She stared at him; he held her gaze, letting her gauge the honesty in his eyes. "If the money's the problem, then I'll tie it up in trust for Tyree."

"And give up that big house of yours?" he asked doubtfully. "Because you know you can't afford to keep it without the income that money provides."

"I'll find a way. I—I could take in boarders to help with the expense, just until the farm starts to pay off." He lifted an eyebrow to let her know what he thought of that, but she wouldn't let go of the notion. "You and the girls could move in! Think how great that would be."

He shook his head, trying hard not to scoff. "Sierra, I can't afford to pay you rent, especially when the girls and I are living rent-free where we are. And who else do you think you're going to get to move all the way out here? I can't think of anyone who would even consider it. Except your ex-husband," he added derisively.

"Like I'd let him anywhere near my place with a suitcase," she muttered, crestfallen. "Dennis is a no-good, fortune-hunting con man."

"Which is exactly what people would be saying about me if we hooked up," Sam pointed out.

"We already are hooked up."

"You know what I mean."

"What I know is that until Edwin Searle took it into his head to write me into his will, Tyree and I weren't so different from you. We were a lot worse off, in fact. We'd been living hand-to-mouth for a long time."

"And you should never have to do that again," he told her. "Believe me when I say that I'm glad you won't."

"But if the money's that big of a problem for you, Sam," she said earnestly, "I don't mind giving it up." He started shaking his head, truly alarmed, but she pressed on. "It wouldn't be for long. You're going to make it big, Sam. I know you are. We are. Together. That's what I came to tell you. We've got an offer, a big one. A wholesaler in Dallas has offered us a contract."

"That's great, but it doesn't really change anything."

"It does! I'm so sure of it that I'll gladly give away every penny of the inheritance if it's that big of a problem for you."

He seized her by the shoulders, needing to know that she heard this, that she believed it. "Listen to me. There is no partnership if you sacrifice your security. Do you hear me? I'm warning you now,

Sierra. I'll walk away without a single look back—
the farm, the partnership, everything—if I so much
as suspect you're even thinking about doing something as stupid as giving your money away. Are you
getting this? Are you?''

Slowly, she nodded, tears filling her eyes.
''You're a good man, Sam.''

''Don't say that.'' Good men didn't use women
for sex, good men didn't let even good sex become
the driving force in their lives, but that's what he
was doing. Wasn't it? He didn't even know anymore.

''You're a better person than I am,'' she insisted.
''In every way that really counts, I'm the one who
doesn't measure up.''

''That's nonsense. Your thinking's screwed up if
you believe that.''

She smiled so sadly that it hurt to see it. ''Then
I'm not so different from you, after all.''

''Different enough,'' he muttered, frowning. His
thinking wasn't screwed up about this. Was it?

She narrowed her eyes, and something within
him, something base and primal, literally rejoiced.
He'd seen that look before. He knew what it meant.
Every part of his body knew what it meant.

''Some differences are good,'' she purred, skim-
ming her hands up his chest to his shoulder. ''In
fact, they're very desirable.''

The next thing he knew, she was pulling off her
sweater and letting it fall away. Once more, no bra,
and once more, he was hard enough in a heartbeat

to do himself bodily harm. He gulped and grabbed on to the remaining shreds of his gallantry.

"We shouldn't be doing this, Sierra."

"Why not? Who are we hurting?"

"Each other."

"That's not how I see it. That's certainly not what it feels like when you're making love to me."

He closed his eyes, but her hands were on him again, gliding over his chest, heating his chilled flesh. He told himself that wanting her this much was downright unnatural. Even a stupid polecat in heat would skedaddle when the headlights of an oncoming car picked him up, but here he stood just watching those headlights speed on, the scent and heat and feel of her stronger than even the instinct for survival.

He just wasn't man enough to walk away from this. That was the painful truth. But when her hands slid down to his belt and tugged, he knew that he was going to let her soothe that pain and every other he had, beginning with the one in his pants. He didn't doubt that he'd pay a price for it later. Still, when she whispered, "Get in the truck, Sam," he did.

And he kept getting in. Deeper and deeper.

Chapter Ten

Mrs. Bailey down at the nursing home died. The poor old thing had been ill for months, so the passing wasn't exactly unexpected, and the family wanted the funeral to take place the very next day. The shop, therefore, was in chaos when Sierra returned that afternoon later than intended.

She didn't get into the actual preparation and arrangement of floral design much these days, choosing instead to concentrate on the bookkeeping and her other business interests. She missed the creative outlet, though, so she didn't hesitate to pitch in. Unfortunately, the time constraints and emotional pressure under which she'd placed herself that day ate up any pleasure she might have taken in the work.

By three-thirty, when she hurried out to pick up Tyree at school, she had a pounding headache, and naturally Tyree didn't want to go back to the shop and quietly do her homework there. Instead, she begged Sierra to let her go to Lana's with the twins. Lana graciously insisted that she wouldn't mind having Tyree over for the afternoon, but Sierra feared what Sam might think about that, so she refused. Tyree sulked, and the two of them argued. That ended with Sierra sending Tyree upstairs to the office alone while she swallowed analgesics and tried to help Bette.

Sierra never had partaken of the lunch she'd had Gwyn pack for her and Sam. Instead, she'd left it with him and hurried back to the shop, having stayed away longer than she'd intended, so when they finally closed up shop that evening, she was starved and her headache was worse. On the way home she decided to swing by the drive-in and pick up a fast-food meal, something she rarely did. Any other time, Tyree would have been thrilled, but not this night. Irritated and impatient, Sierra snapped at the child, so by the time they got home, wagging a sackful of hamburgers and fries, both were in a foul mood.

It was the worst possible time to find a special delivery on their doorstep. After dragging the big box inside, she opened the top and went through the contents, finding toys, clothing and compact discs.

"I cannot believe you've done this," Sierra

scolded, holding her head. "We discussed this, Tyree."

"It's my birthday stuff!" Tyree exclaimed, as if that explained everything.

"I didn't give you permission to order these things."

"But Daddy did! These are from him, my birthday gifts from *him*."

Sierra rolled her eyes, her head pounding like someone was using a sledgehammer on her skull. "Your father has no right to give you permission to spend money that isn't his!"

"He promised to pay you back as soon as he can afford it."

"Oh, for pity's sake, Tyree!" Sierra exploded. "Your father will never be able to afford these things, and he never intends to pay back the money! This is his way of punishing me for being more fortunate than he is!"

"That's not so!" Tyree bawled. "Daddy loves me! He wants me to have this stuff for my birthday."

"Then let him buy it," Sierra said, closing up the box again, "because this is going back first thing in the morning."

"No!"

"Yes! First thing. I'm sorry, Tyree, but I just can't allow this to go on. Dennis should never have encouraged you to spend money like this, and since it's not fair to expect you to be more responsible than he is, I'm also canceling our Internet account and every credit card you may have the number of."

Tyree reeled back, tears streaming down her face. "No, Mommy! Please!"

"I have no choice," Sierra said flatly. "I should have done it sooner."

"But they're Daddy's birthday gifts to me! Why are you being so mean?"

Sierra had had enough. "Go to your room," she instructed sternly. "I'll bring your dinner up once you've calmed down. Now march!"

Tyree ran for the stairs, sobbing. Sierra bowed her head, which felt as if it was splitting in two. She hoped she wasn't coming down with something, because she just didn't think she could deal with an illness right now. She had her hands full with Tyree and Dennis. And Sam.

She wanted nothing so much as she wanted Sam then. What she wouldn't give just to feel his arms around her! She needed his steadying influence, his calm good sense. She should've listened to him when he'd first suggested that she cancel the Internet account, but she'd been too stubborn and foolish then to appreciate his obvious wisdom. Now Sam was being the stubborn, foolish one. Would the day come when they could be wise together?

"You girls okay in there?" Sam asked through the bathroom door.

He hadn't had to worry about leaving them alone in the bath for a long time now, but some habits died hard.

"We're okay, Sam," the girls shouted in unison, followed by lots of giggling and some splashes.

"Just holler if you need anything."

He headed back to the kitchen to finish putting away the dinner dishes. As he worked, he wondered what Sierra was doing. The girls had wanted to go over to Tyree's this evening, and he'd almost given in. It had been a while since they'd had one of Sierra's good home-cooked meals, and he missed the laughs they'd all shared, but since things had heated up between him and Sierra, he hadn't been comfortable hanging around her house with the girls. It was too hard to keep his hands off her. Still, he couldn't help wondering what she and Tyree were up to.

A bang on the door interrupted his thoughts, and he closed the cabinet, curiosity propelling him past the small dining table and across the neat but threadbare living room to the front door. He opened it and nearly fell over when Tyree burst into the room and threw her arms around his waist.

"Tyree? What're you doing here?" He looked out the door, dread filling him, but it was not Sierra's automobile that sat running in the road in front of his house. It was a familiar battered truck. "Is that Terry Zimmerman?" The Zimmerman kid lived with his parents a few miles up the road.

Instead of answering him, Tyree waved to the teenager. He waved back and took off. Sam turned Tyree to face him and saw the dirty tear tracks on her face.

"What's going on? Did Terry bring you here?"

She nodded sullenly. "I'm not going back. It's awful there. She's mad at me again." She pushed hair out of her face and sniffed.

"Have you run away?" he asked her, already knowing the answer.

Her bottom lip quivered. "Can I stay here?"

"No," he told her flatly.

"Then take me to my daddy!"

Sam put a hand between her shoulder blades and ushered her, none too gently, into the house, closing the door behind her. "I'm not taking you anywhere until I find out what's going on." He took her coat off her, tossed it over a chair and marched her to the couch, where he sat her down, saying sternly, "Don't you move a muscle until I get back."

He went into the kitchen to telephone Sierra, who wasn't at home. No doubt she was out looking for her daughter, so he left a message on the machine and called her cell phone. She answered on the second ring with Tyree's name. Calmly, he let her know that the child was safe with him. He didn't argue when she said that she was on her way, just told her to drive safely and got off the line. Maybe it was better if she saw just how differently they lived. Walking down the hall, he tapped on the bathroom door, then stuck his head inside, finding the twins all wrapped up in towels and brushing their teeth.

"When you two are through in here, I want you to go to your room and get dressed for bed, then wait there for me. We've got a situation going out here. Tyree's in the living room."

"Tyree?" Kim piped up eagerly, but Sam shook his head.

"She's run away from home and turned up here. I'm going to have to pin her ears back, so you two keep shy of the situation until I tell you otherwise. Okay?"

They exchanged a wide-eyed look, then both nodded.

"I'll fill you in later," he promised with a wink before closing the door.

He stepped across the hall and into the living room. Tyree sat on the edge of the couch right where he'd left her. She was frowning and swinging her feet nervously. He pulled a footstool over in front of her and sat down.

"Let's have it, and be quick about it."

Tyree's chin trembled. "She's making me send my birthday presents back and closing off the computer account."

"You bought something else when you knew you weren't supposed to, didn't you?"

She folded her arms mulishly and slumped back onto the couch. "Daddy said I could. For my birthday."

"Did you use your daddy's credit card this time?"

Her eyes filled up. "He doesn't have any."

"Then he's got no business giving you permission to shop on the Internet."

She rubbed tears from her cheeks and said, "But if I don't, he'll go away again." The words came out strangled and whiny.

Sam kept his reaction minimal. "He tell you that?"

She shook her head, and her face contorted with fresh tears. "But I know it. He didn't come back 'til we got the money."

Sobbing, she reached out, and Sam went onto his knees, hugging her close. He'd have gladly put a fist in Dennis Carlton's face about then, if for no other reason than because he hadn't made this little girl believe that he loved her.

"Now you listen to me, cupcake. Maybe he didn't come around so much until your mom inherited all that money, but he loves you. Any daddy would love a little girl like you."

"Would you, Sam?" she asked, the little hitch in her voice plucking at his heartstrings.

"Yes, ma'am, but that doesn't mean I wouldn't do exactly what your mom did, Tyree, and, girl, if you had run away from me, you'd be grounded until you're old enough to drive, I swear. Speaking of which, where the heck did you find Terry Zimmerman?"

She hitched a shoulder and sat back glumly. "I was just walking along the road, and he stopped." Sam felt a chill crawl up his spine, but she went on innocently, "When he asked where I live, I just told him I live here."

Sam slapped a hand over the gooseflesh prickling the nape of his neck. "You are one lucky kid," he told her, getting to his feet. "What if the person who had stopped and picked you up was a criminal, Tyree? What if he'd hurt you or just driven away

with you in the car? We'd never even know what
had happened to you. Can you imagine what that
would do to your mom and dad? It would kill your
mother, Tyree. Believe me. It would kill her.''

Tyree started to cry again, sobbing against her
knees, but Sam didn't cut her any slack.

''Besides that, girl, you're just plain wrong. I
know you love your dad, and I can't imagine that
he doesn't love you, but when he gets you to buy
stuff for him on your mom's credit card that's the
next thing to stealing. Your mom has every right to
get upset about that.''

''But we've got lots of money,'' Tyree cried, trying to sound pathetic.

''So what? The store's got lots of candy. Would
it be all right for you to get the little girl of the
store's owner to sneak some out to you without her
mom's permission?''

She looked up at him, and he could tell that she
was trying to come up with an answer for that
which would help her case, but she couldn't, so in
the end she just put her head down against her
knees again.

''I'll tell you something else while I'm at it,'' he
went on. ''Your mom doesn't have as much money
as you seem to think she does.'' Tyree's head came
up at that, so he explained. ''She spent a good
chunk of her inheritance on that house of yours, and
she invested a whole bunch more in the farm.
What's left is generating income so she can keep
that house going and provide for you, though if you
ask me, she does way too much of that.''

Tyree frowned, not liking that a bit, but that was just too bad. This little gal had a few things to learn, and if her mother couldn't get through to her, then he'd have to do it.

"See, it's not good to have everything you want, because then you don't have anything to look forward to, and that's bound to make you unhappy. It's good to have goals, to be working toward something or looking forward to something. If you get it all too quick, then you're just sitting there wondering what's next. It's better to enjoy one thing at a time and look forward to the next. Your mom's right to cut off your access to those Internet shopping sites because things aren't going to make you happy, Tyree. You've got plenty of things already, but here you sit bawling like a newborn calf that can't find its mama's teat."

She blinked at that, solemn-faced. He rubbed a hand over the top of her dark red head, and that's when they heard the car pull up into the drive.

"Is that Mom?" she asked warily.

"Most likely. I suggest you get on an apology binge right quick."

Tyree nodded and Sam stepped outside to greet Sierra, who practically flew across his yard. He had no time to worry about what she'd think of the place. Her haggard, bedraggled appearance prompted him to open his arms. She threw herself into them, trembling so hard from the evening chill and emotional shock that her teeth chattered.

"Is she all right?"

"She's fine."

Sierra immediately drew back. "When I think what could have happened!"

"I know. Me, too."

He turned and walked her toward the house, his arm about her. She was still trembling when he let go of her so she could pass through the door.

Tyree had come to her feet and stood uncertainly in front of the couch, hands nervously fiddling with the hem of her sweater. Sierra took one look at her and ran across the room to scoop the girl into her arms.

"You scared me!"

"I'm sorry!"

"You could've been lost or killed."

"I know."

Sierra stood the girl on her feet again and bent to bring her face on level with Tyree's. "What were you thinking?"

Tyree shrugged. "I was just mad 'cause you took everything away."

Sierra bit her lip, and Sam could see her resolve fading, so he quickly stepped in. "Your mom was exactly right in doing that, Tyree," he said, "and you know why because we've already talked about it."

Tyree bowed her head, and Sierra shot a look over her shoulder at Sam before addressing her daughter once more. "I'm so glad you're safe. I never want you to take this sort of chance again, but the gifts go back and the Internet account is canceled. For now."

"And you're going to spend a week without TV, too," Sam put in.

Tyree gasped, and Sierra looked over at him in surprise, but at his nod, she took a deep breath and stiffened her spine. "A week," she confirmed, "because what you did was so very dangerous."

Tyree hung her head sullenly, tears rolling down her nose. "No gifts, no Internet, no TV. Daddy prob'ly won't even come to my birthday party, either."

Sierra folded her arms, her countenance hardening. "That may be for the best. In fact, I'm not sure he should even be invited."

Tyree's head came up, eyes wide and flashing with temper.

"Of course her father'll be invited to her birthday party," Sam said firmly. "Whether he comes or not, that's up to him."

Tyree shot him a grateful look, and Sierra reluctantly nodded, obviously understanding what he'd been trying to tell her. If Tyree was going to be disappointed, let it be by her father.

"Sam is right," Sierra said. "I won't keep your dad from coming to your birthday party."

Tyree nodded glumly and fidgeted, pressing her legs together. "I need to go to the bathroom."

Sam pointed to the hallway door. "Straight across."

"Wash your hands when you're done," Sierra instructed. Tyree nodded and hurried from the room. When she was gone, Sierra looked at Sam. "I should've known she'd come to you."

"A neighbor kid of mine gave her a lift, Terry Zimmerman. No doubt she knew I'd call you the minute she showed up, which just goes to prove that she didn't really want to run away from home. She was just trying to scare you, I figure."

"It worked."

"Yeah, well, I think she scared herself pretty good, too. She didn't squawk much when I gave her a tongue-lashing."

Sierra looked up at him. "Maybe, deep down, that's just what she needs."

"What that girl needs," he told her unthinkingly, "is a father more concerned about her than what he can get out of her."

"Like you, in other words. She needs a father like you." Sierra tilted her head, piercing him with her gaze. "Seems we both need a man like you in our lives."

Sam felt a strange, crowding sensation in his chest, as if his heart literally swelled. Could that be true? Was it possible that it was more than just Sierra, that they both actually needed him, not just on the farm but in their lives? He swallowed a lump in his throat.

"About that TV thing. I shouldn't have butted in."

"No, you were right. What she did was extremely dangerous, but I'm not sure she understands that. A week without television might make her think twice before she does something like this again."

Sam nodded and slipped his fingertips into the

back pockets of his jeans. His impulse was to walk across the room and hug her, but he'd just wind up kissing her, and now was not the time. Proving that, Tyree returned just then.

"Can I go say hi to Kim and Keli?"

Sierra shook her head. "Not tonight. We haven't even had supper yet. You can see Kim and Keli tomorrow at school."

"Maybe they could come home with you after school," Sam suggested, looking at Sierra, letting her know with his eyes that this was for him, for the two of them.

"Oh, Mom, can they? Please? I'm sorry I took off. I won't do it again, ever, I swear."

Sierra smiled, then looked down at her daughter. "No TV," she warned, "and homework first. I mean it." Tyree nodded eagerly. Sierra looked at Sam, smiling again. "I'll pick up the girls from school then."

"I'll let Lana know."

The warmth in Sierra's hazel eyes filled him with all kinds of silly thoughts, hopeful, foolish notions that he'd held at bay until now. He saw them out, listened to the sounds of her tires as they drove away and rubbed a hand over his chin.

Could it work? He had two little girls who could never be treated as equals to Tyree when it came to clothing and other things. Unless Sierra was willing to set some real firm boundaries with Tyree. God knew it wouldn't do the girl any harm. On the other hand, if his own income increased, they'd be on a more equal footing. What he'd said to Tyree about her mom not having as much money as it seemed was dead-on, but the gulf between them was still large. Could he close it? If he worked real hard, could he make the farm a big enough success that Sierra wouldn't need to live on the income generated by her inheritance?

He couldn't quite convince himself that it was possible, but it couldn't hurt to try. The farm was going to pay—he believed that with his whole being—but could he turn it into the phenomenally successful venture that he needed to make this work with Sierra?

Well, he decided, turning his steps toward the twins' bedroom, it wouldn't be for lack of trying. No more distractions. It was time to get down to real business. He was going to hit the books again, learn everything he could about growing and selling flowers, then he was going to do his best to put that knowledge to work for them, not just for *the* future, but for *their* future. Together.

Chapter Eleven

"It's a big risk," Sierra said, "signing a contract with a wholesaler." She watched from her desk chair as Sam bent over her desk and signed his name to the contract.

"I know it is, sweetheart, but if we can keep up our end of the bargain, it'll pay off real handsome."

She hugged that endearment close, wondering if he realized how often he called her by pet names lately. Sweetheart. Honey. Darlin'. The words were always tossed out casually, but they could mean that he was coming to care for her in a special way. Or did they?

She shook herself, fighting to pay attention. "You're right, of course. I can hardly believe the wholesaler is willing to take a chance on us like this.''

''That's your doing,'' Sam said, parking himself on the corner of her desk and smiling warmly. ''You sold them on S & S Farms.''

''But if we should fail, Sam…''

''I'm not going to let that happen. We're going to fill this contract, and the next one's going to be even bigger. You mark my words on that.''

She believed him. He'd worked like a Trojan lately, daylight to dark, as if his life depended on the success of S & S Farms, and more often than not they spent the evening together. He still went home every night, but at least once or twice a week the twins stayed over, and on those occasions they found a way to be together, sometimes downstairs, sometimes in the guest room, sometimes making use of dark corners and their imaginations.

In general, their lovemaking had become quick and intense and always occurred at night. Sam was working so hard these days to fulfil the wholesale contract that he almost seemed obsessed, as if he just couldn't tear himself away from the farm. Sierra was becoming concerned. She loved him desperately and knew that they belonged together; she was even beginning to believe that it might happen, but she had started to worry about why they might wind up together permanently.

It was ironic, really. Once she'd have used any means to prevent him from keeping distance between them. She'd even bartered her body for the chance to stay close to Sam, to make him see that they should be together. Now she was afraid that what had convinced Sam was not how good they were together but how much he figured that she and Tyree and the farm needed him. And that wasn't good enough. It wasn't the money that could keep them apart, though that obviously remained a big obstacle for Sam, and it wasn't the piddling age difference. What it all boiled down to was whether or not Sam loved her.

Oh, he made love to her wonderfully well, and he cared for her, just as he cared for Tyree. Sam was a caring man, too caring, perhaps. He thought he had to fix everything and everybody. His early experience had insured that. He'd tried to take care of his mother, to stand between her and her abusive husband, but in the end he'd had to leave to keep a bad situation from escalating, and that one failure had shaped Sam for life. The way he took care of the girls, Tyree, her, everyone, all came back to that one experience.

Now he was doing it again, taking care of her and Tyree, providing the guidance and strength they both needed. They needed stability; he was giving it to them. She wanted to prove that she could make the right choices, handle her finances, and he was making that possible, too. She threw herself into his arms, practically begged him to make love to her, and he put her into orbit every time. But did he love her? Was she anything to him like he was to her? Or was she another obligation, another soul in need of rescue? Nothing had ever terrified Sierra more than that thought did.

"This calls for a celebration," Sam declared, clapping his hands together.

Sierra blinked, momentarily unable to find anything to celebrate in this situation, then she remembered the contract. "Oh. Do you think so?"

"Absolutely." He grinned ear to ear. "How about we drive into Fort Worth for dinner? There's a steak house on the south side where they have a dance band and an indoor playground with a big slide that dumps you right onto the dance floor. I took the twins on their last birthday, and they loved it."

Sierra nodded and punched up her smile. "Sounds like fun."

"Great." He rocked onto his feet, bent and dropped a kiss onto the center of her forehead, just as if she were one of the girls. "Better get going. Lots to do. I'll change at your place. Save time that way." He headed for the door. "Be ready when I come in, okay? And wear your dancing shoes."

"We'll be ready," Sierra promised.

He tossed her a wink as he headed out the door.

Sierra closed her eyes as soon as he was out of sight. She had never felt less like dancing in her life.

"You don't have to go up if you don't want to, baby," Sam said to Kim. Kim was a little frightened of slides, given her past experience. Keli and

Tyree had no such compunctions, however, and were already standing in line.

"Will you come with me?" she asked.

"Sure, if that's what you want." He looked at Sierra and added, "We both will."

Sierra looked at the height of that slide, fifteen feet at least, and her hand went automatically to her belly. "I don't think I'd better."

Sam's face clouded. "What's the matter, honey, you feeling bad?"

She dropped her hand and pushed aside a tiny burst of panic. "Just a little squeamish."

He stepped close and slid an arm around her. "Why didn't you say so? If you're coming down with something, we can go on home. The food hasn't even come yet."

She shook her head and pasted on a smile, feeling like the world's worst liar. "No, no. I—I think the problem is that I'm starving. I skipped lunch today."

"Silly girl," he said, hooking an arm around her neck and drawing her in for a quick kiss. Kim giggled behind her cupped hand. Sam looked down at her. "What're you laughing at, kiddo? You're next."

Releasing Sierra, he swept up Kim, kissing her all over her face. People in the noisy, busy restaurant stopped what they were doing to watch and smile, including the other girls, who hopped up and down, calling for Kim as they shuffled forward in the line for the slide.

Sam carried her toward them, but at the last moment he looked over his shoulder at Sierra, instructing, "Have some of that hot bread the waitress just brought to the table. Maybe it'll settle your stomach."

Sierra nodded and smiled. There he went again, taking care of everyone, making her love him more and more. If only she could be sure that he loved her, too. She wanted, needed, to be everything to him that he was to her. The fear that she might have trapped them both was eating her alive.

"Hey!" Sam called, standing in the doorway to the den, a clean change of clothing rolled into a bundle beneath one arm. He'd started cleaning up at Sierra's. It was more comfortable and more convenient than waiting until he got home, which was sometimes very late, indeed, especially on a Saturday night like this one. "Where is everyone?"

Giggles wafted tinnily out of the distance, and he turned his head to look at the intercom on the wall.

"Upstairs!" Tyree answered through the small microphone.

In the background he could hear the twins squealing, "Get ready! Get ready!"

Sam shook his head, grinning as he made his way to the stairs and climbed them. About the time he set his foot on the landing, he heard music in Sierra's room. It was the girls' favorite place to play. His, too, come to think of it. Though he and Sierra had only made love once on that wonderful, big bed of hers, he often dreamed about being there with her. He walked along the landing to the open doorway, poking his head through. Someone had moved the bedside lamps, tilting the shades so that the light was thrown onto a spot just beyond the foot of the bed. A chair had been placed several feet away. The room, however, was empty.

"I'm here. Where're ya'll?"

Giggles emanated from the large, opulent bath and dressing area. Suddenly the dressing room door flew open and Tyree pranced out, swathed head to foot in shiny, dark green fabric. Her hair had been scooped up on top of her head and she wore elaborate eye makeup and bright lipstick. She carried a round shampoo bottle upside down in one hand by its long cap.

"Ladies and gentlemen in the audience," she announced in a loud, almost shrill voice, "the fashion show is ready. Please sit down." She stabbed a finger repeatedly at the chair in the center of the floor.

Concluding that he was the "audience," Sam strode over and obediently dropped down into the chair, placing his bundle on the floor.

"Oh, boy," he said loudly, knowing how they loved to play dress-up, "a fashion show." He'd teased them before about being models, and now they were taking the game to the next logical step.

Tyree sashayed forward, every step a miracle of accomplishment, considering the too-large high heels she was wearing with yards and yards of dress. "The announcer," she shrieked, meaning herself, obviously, "is wearing a forest bridemaid dress with a real full skirt and glamorous shoes."

Sam bit the inside of his cheek to keep from laughing at her phraseology. She hit the light mark on the floor and spun around, nearly toppling over. A hank of hair fell down over her face, but she just pushed it back and hitched up the belt holding everything in place.

"She has jewelry," Tyree went on loudly, speaking into the bottom of the shampoo bottle and tugging at the long string of cultured pearls looped around her neck, "that's, uh, very, very long."

"Yeah!" Sam applauded vigorously.

"Next is Keli!" Tyree screamed.

Keli practically fell into the room, wearing a veil pinned to her hair and giggling almost uncontrollably, but Tyree didn't let that affect her monologue.

"Supermodel Keli is wearing hair pants and—"

"Harem pants!" Sierra hissed from the bathroom, and Sam clamped a hand over his mouth to hold back the laughter tearing up his eyes.

"Hair-em pants," Tyree continued, "with a vest and scarf and lots of coins and chains." The cobbled together costume was anything but sultry, especially when Keli made a giggling attempt at a belly dance in a vest that hung down to mid-thigh. Sierra had wrapped cords around the bottoms of the pants legs to hold them up. "Oh, and sandals," Tyree added belatedly, as Keli was already running away from the spotlight. She plopped on the bed, laughing merrily.

Kim was next, of course, in silk pajamas, flip-flops and some pieces of jade jewelry. Sierra had lined her eyes to make them look slanted and combed her blond bangs and hair down straight. She took mincing little steps, kept her hands pressed together in front of her and bowed repeatedly while Tyree shouted about the Oriental look.

"It's, uh, Japany silk," she said proudly, "made with real worms."

Sam nearly fell off his chair, howling. He could hear Sierra sputtering in the bathroom.

"Well, it is," Kim insisted indignantly, hands at her hips. "It's made from silkworms. Sierra said so."

Sam controlled his laughter long enough to applaud. He stood for good measure, and Kim took a pleased bow.

He figured the show was over at that, but Tyree lifted an arm and slung it at the dressing room door, yelling, "Sierra the beautiful!"

Sam dropped back down into his chair, eager for the final act. Sierra stepped into the doorway and struck a Gloria Swanson pose, one arm stretched upward against the doorjamb, one leg thrust to the side. She wore a V-necked, sleeveless silver-gray sheath, and a long, narrow scarf with fringed ends wound about her throat. Her hair had been tamed into a bun at the nape of her neck, and she wore a second scarf around her forehead and tied in a bow beneath the bun. Red lipstick, penciled brows, a clunky bracelet, bare legs and high heels completed the ensemble.

"This is the thirty movie-star look," Tyree announced. "A flapped dress and elegant 'cessories."

Sam grinned as Sierra waltzed around the room. God, she was beautiful. Elegant accessories, indeed. He followed her with his eyes, wanting her with a very pleasant ache. Happiness wrapped around him. Despite all the work, all the worry, all the doubts, all the fears, he'd never been happier than he was right here, right now with his girls showing off for him. His girls.

His woman.

At least for now.

"That's it for our fashion show," Tyree cried, waving frantically for Keli and Kim to fall in beside Sierra for the big finale.

They lined up like cancan dancers, arms linked, with Tyree on one end and Sierra on the other. Sierra counted under her breath, and when she reached three, they all bowed. Tyree overdid it, throwing out the arm with the shampoo bottle. She stumbled, got caught in her skirts and went down. Sam immediately jumped up and started applauding wildly, hooting and whistling.

Laughing, the twins fell on top of Tyree, pulling Sierra down with them. Soon they were all laughing, filling the room with great delighted whoops.

"Bravo! Bravo!" Sam called, still clapping.

Delighted with themselves, the girls began thanking Sierra for helping them by covering her with kisses, leaving bright red lip prints all over her face. Sam decided that he had to get in on that. Going down on his knees, he grabbed two of the girls by the ankles and pulled them off Sierra, then fell on top of her with a growl. The girls launched themselves at the kissing couple, squealing with glee. He thought his chest might burst with sheer joy.

He finally had to come up for air, and got his face smacked by the girls for it. Rolling himself into a sitting position, he put his back to the end of the bed and caught his breath, pulling Sierra up beside him. She'd lost the scarf tied around her head and her hair was loosening from its bun. He couldn't resist getting a hand into it.

"Whoo-ee! Best fashion show ever," he pronounced.

"Oh, Sam," Keli said, sitting up with an ear-to-ear grin and pushing hair out of her eyes.

"That was fun!" Kim exclaimed.

Tyree dropped the shampoo bottle and started getting out of her gear. "You said we were good models, and I guess we are."

"You sure are," Sam agreed, smiling so wide his face hurt.

Sierra scooted up underneath his arm and sighed contentedly. "They worked all afternoon to get this ready for you."

"Well, it was sure worth it," he said, looking down at her, "but I have an idea who did most of the work."

"You did great, Mom," Tyree agreed. "Thanks for helping us."

"Yeah, thanks," the twins echoed, and they both scrambled over to wrap their arms around Sierra and kiss her again. She hugged them tight, smiling fondly.

Tyree just watched, pushing down the "forest bridemaid dress" and stepping out of it. "That thing's hot," she said.

"I remember thinking the same thing at my cousin's wedding," Sierra told her, with the twins snuggled down at her side.

"What's for dinner?" Tyree suddenly wanted to know. "Dressing up makes you hungry!"

"Nothing fancy," Sierra announced, starting to get up.

Sam beat her to it and reached down a hand for her. She took it, and he hauled her up and against him, wanting very much to wrap his arms around her and kiss her again as he had earlier. Well, not quite. Kim was in the way, however, and Sierra quickly sidestepped to avoid knocking her down, saying, "You girls get changed and washed up. Be sure to put everything away."

The three girls hurried to the bathroom, Tyree carrying several yards of the forest-green dress. Sierra smiled at Sam.

"I'll jump into some jeans and start dinner."

He shook his head. "You don't have to do that. It's late to be starting to cook. Besides, you make dinner for me and the twins too often as it is. We'll pick up something on the way home.''

''Don't be silly,'' Sierra told him, unwinding the scarf about her neck and starting toward the dressing room. ''There isn't a thing between here and your house. Besides, as much fun as I have with the girls, one of my greatest joys is putting a meal on the table for the people I love.'' She smiled and closed the dressing room door.

Sam stood there an instant longer, his heart in his throat. Then he sat down again in that chair, closed his eyes and pressed his hands together, savoring what had to be one of the sweetest moments of his life.

After the room cleared, Sam showered and changed in the master bath, then went down to join the others. The smell of frying bacon filled the air. He sometimes made breakfast for dinner himself, so he assumed that was what was afoot. Instead, he found the girls happily building BLTs with slices of potato bread, tomato, lettuce and cheese.

''We're having a fat feast,'' Sierra said, licking her fingers after piling crisp bacon onto her sandwich. She had fried a mountain of the stuff.

Sam raised his eyebrows. Sierra usually ate very moderately, but that sandwich was the size of a football. She plopped bread onto the top of it, squished it down with her hand and picked it up, tearing into it with uncustomary gusto. She closed her eyes.

''Mmm.''

Sam laughed, glad to see her enjoyment of the monster. He started building his own, filching sliced cucumber in the process. At least she hadn't added insult to injury by putting out potato chips. He was pleased to see that the girls had restricted themselves to two or three slices of bacon each for their sandwiches. He followed suit, figuring he could allow himself two sandwiches that way, but he hadn't even got the top on the first one when Sierra dropped hers, slapped a hand over her mouth and bolted.

"Sierra? Honey?"

Ignoring him, she tore through the dining room and out into the hall to the powder room. She was puking into the toilet when he caught up with her.

"Oh, honey, you're sick. Here, let me help you." He ripped a hand towel from a ring attached to the wall and wet it beneath the spigot in the sink. After wringing it out, he folded it and draped it over the nape of her neck, then reached around to feel her forehead. She felt cold and clammy, not feverish. "I'm going to call the doc."

"No," she gasped. "Just get out."

"I don't like you being sick like this."

"Go away, Sam."

"Let me help you, honey. I don't mind."

"Get out, Sam!" she gritted through her teeth.

Figuring she was embarrassed, he backed off. "Okay. Fine." He backed out into the hall.

"Close the door," she instructed, still bent over the toilet.

He closed the door. Maybe she was coming down with something, and if she was, the girls would be, too. They were kissing all over each other earlier, after all. He walked back to the kitchen.

"How's everybody in here?" The girls looked up from the stools they'd arranged around the center island.

"Is Mom okay?" Tyree asked lightly.

"I think maybe all that bacon grease made her a little sick," he said. "How about you three? Any queasy stomachs?"

They all shook their heads. "These are good," Kim said behind her hand so that he wouldn't see her full mouth.

"Yeah, but they're treacherous. Too much fat and other bad stuff."

"Guess that's why Mom never made them before," Tyree said, taking a big bite of hers.

Sam washed his hands and finished building his own sandwich, saying, "I'm kind of surprised she made them now, but I guess once won't hurt."

"She said she had a craving for bacon and tomato," Tyree revealed.

Sam glanced through the dining room at that closed powder room door, seeming to remember that she'd been nauseated once before and wondering if he should check on her again. He looked to Tyree. "She been feeling okay?"

Tyree shrugged. "Guess so."

Maybe the bacon was off, he thought. He picked up his sandwich and took a bite of it, judging the flavor. If anything was wrong, he sure couldn't tell. He looked at that door again. "Maybe we ought to make her some hot tea. I've always heard hot tea was good for the stomach."

"I'll put on some water," Tyree said, putting down her sandwich and getting off the stool. Sam divided his attention between Tyree and that rest room door. When the kettle was on the burner and the flame carefully adjusted beneath it, Tyree returned to her meal.

Sam made quick work of his sandwich, so when Sierra finally emerged, his hands were free. He wiped his hands and mouth and went to her. "How're you feeling, honey?"

She smiled wanly and nodded. Her face was splotched and her eyes were red, as if she'd been crying. "I think I'm okay now. It's been so hectic that I haven't been eating regularly, and when I'm really hungry my stomach seems to fill up with too much acid and whatever hits it first comes right back up."

"That what happened the other night?"

She nodded, turning away. "I guess the greasy bacon got to me this time."

He stepped up behind her and began massaging her shoulders, saying, "I want you to take better care of yourself. You don't need to be missing meals. Tyree and I are making you a nice hot cup of tea. Maybe that'll settle your stomach."

"That's sweet, but I don't think I can manage the tea."

"No problem. What would you like?" He stopped the massage, ready to serve her.

"Milk," she said decidedly, still not quite looking at him. "Milk and tomatoes."

He lifted his eyebrows at that. "O-kay. Whatever works. But are you sure that's what you really want? I mean, if you're coming down with a stomach virus, I'm not sure that's the best combination. Crackers and tea might be easier on you."

"It's not a stomach virus," she told him rather impatiently. "I told you. It's happened before. I wait too long to eat, my stomach fills up with acid. Whatever hits it first comes right back up."

"But milk and tomatoes?"

"The milk will, like, coat my stomach, and the tomato acid will sort of offset what I've already got going. Besides, it just sounds good."

He got her the milk and tomatoes, watching with bemused interest as she salted the tomatoes and washed them down with the cold milk. Afterward, to his surprise, she seemed fine.

"You're sure you're okay now?"

"Excellent."

"And you're going to start taking better care of yourself?"

She looked away. "I'll start eating regularly. You don't have to worry about me, Sam. I can take care of myself."

"Maybe I like to take care of you," he said with a shrug.

She looked at him then. "You like to take care of everyone, Sam. It's what you do."

He couldn't imagine why that made her feel so sad, but he couldn't mistake that look on her face. No matter what she said, she couldn't be feeling too good. "I think I'll stay over tonight, sleep on the couch, just in case you need anything."

She closed her eyes and nodded. "In that case, I think I'll turn in early."

He gave her a quick hug. "You do that. I'll take care of the girls and the cleaning up."

She moved away quickly, and later when he went up to check on her, she seemed to be sleeping soundly. He went back down the stairs thinking that one day, if all went well, they wouldn't have to sleep apart. Then he could take care of the woman he loved all the time.

Chapter Twelve

"How're you feeling?"

"I'm fine." She was always fine in the morning, even this early, but while she was feeling particularly rested and well, Sam looked tired standing there in her kitchen. "How did you sleep?"

"Okay."

"I wish you didn't have to stay on that couch when you're here."

"Me, too, but it can't be helped. Listen, if you're okay, I'll head out now. Want to get an early start today."

"It's Sunday, Sam," Sierra told him, her voice containing the edge of a scold.

"I know that, honey, but this is a busy time. We're about to start planting."

She nodded reluctantly. "Did you at least eat something?"

"Yeah, cereal and milk. Made some coffee, too. Want me to pour you a cup? You're looking pretty sleepy there, pretty cute, too, but pretty sleepy."

She wrinkled her nose. "Maybe later. Do you really have to work today, Sam?"

"Yeah, I'm afraid I do."

"Can I help at all?"

"Just keep an eye on the girls today. Tomorrow, though, you might start trying to hire us some help around here. We've got acres of seedlings to plant, and one pair of hands won't get it done."

Sierra thought that over. "Will you be wanting to interview prospective employees?"

"Nope. I'll leave that to you. Just remember that it's dirty, backbreaking work, not particularly difficult but with lots of bending and stooping involved. I'd go for any age, so long as they have the dexterity to get the job done, and a love of gardening would be a plus."

"I'll place some ads and contact a few employment offices today. How many do you need and when do you want them to start?"

"I could use one or two right away and, say, four or five more within the next three weeks."

"I'll get right on it, but I warn you, it's going to take a week or so."

"That's okay. I'll manage."

"Maybe you can take a day off now and again if I get you some help."

He jerked his head. "It's going to be daylight to

dark for the foreseeable future, I'm afraid. Once I see we're going to meet that contract, then I can slack off, but not before. Oh, one more thing.''

''Yeah?''

''Make sure that whoever you hire and whatever age they are that they know who the boss is.''

Sierra rolled her eyes. ''Sam, no one will ever doubt who the boss is around S & S Farms.''

''I meant you, sweetheart.''

''Sam,'' she repeated drolly, ''no one will ever doubt who the boss is around S & S Farms. And I don't mean me.'' She stepped close, placing her hands on his chest, and looked up at him. ''Just so you know, I wouldn't have it any other way.''

Grinning, he bent and kissed her lingeringly on the mouth. ''Eat,'' he ordered before he went out to take on the day.

Sierra lay on Sam's chest, the top of her head tucked beneath his chin. His hand made lazy circles on her back.

They'd dressed again after making love in case one of the girls should come downstairs for something, but Sierra had convinced Sam to stay over once more. He had worked so hard and seemed so tired that she hadn't wanted him on the road. He was insistent, however, that he would sleep on the couch, while she went upstairs to sleep in the guest room alone. It didn't matter that he would be up and out before the girls so much as turned over in the morning. Sam had his principles, and he wouldn't let his sisters catch him sleeping with their best friend's mother, even if he and Sierra already were a couple in the girls' eyes. So here they lay on the couch in the den, stacked like a layer cake, sexual satisfaction between them. Sexual but none other.

Sierra closed her eyes, aching with what was in her heart.

"Sam," she asked softly, trying to keep the tremor out of her voice, "have you ever thought about having children of your own?"

His hand never stopped its lazy circuit, drawing comfort and contentment on her back. "As far as I'm concerned, I already have children of my own."

"I know. I meant, more children. Have you ever thought of having more children?"

"Sure. Some day. When I can afford it."

Sierra bit her lip. The urge to let it be was powerful, but she just couldn't.

"I think I may have left Tyree alone too long," she said. "I never wanted her to be an only child like I was. I've spoiled her. If I'd had another child, I might've had an easier time dealing with her."

"And you might not have," Sam rebutted gently, and his hand finally stopped its ministrations. She missed it instantly. "You never know about those things, Sierra. Besides, Tyree's going to be fine. You say she's spoiled, and maybe she is in a way, but she's also generous, and she never lords it over the twins like some kids in her position would. She's got a good heart. Maybe she's a little headstrong, but that's okay. We all get to be who we are, you know, for the most part.''

Sierra smiled against his chest. "Do you know how wonderful you are?''

He looked down, drawing his chin to his collarbone. "I don't think I'm wonderful. You've got no idea how I struggle to do right. We're proof that I too often fail.''

"Don't say that," she protested, rising up onto her forearms so she could look him in the face. "You're just about the best thing that's ever happened to me. That's not wrong.''

He lifted his hand to her hair, cupping the back of her head. "Okay, but it is hypocrisy.''

"How so?''

"Because, honey, if you were one of the girls, I'd want to kill me.''

"Oh, Sam, no.''

"I mean it, Sierra. I want my girls settled with men who love them but will also do right by them, men who can pull their own weight. Why do you think I've struggled so much with this?''

Sierra bowed her head, tears filling her eyes. He had as much as said that he didn't love her. She gulped, trying not to weep. All along he'd said that he wasn't the man for her, presumably because he couldn't "pull his own weight," as he put it. The truth seemed to be, however, that he just couldn't love her the way she loved him, and she couldn't even blame him for it. All Sam had done was let himself be seduced. No, she only had herself to blame for this fiasco. And yet he cared on some level; she knew that he did. Unfortunately, if she wound up with Sam permanently, it would be more a matter of him "doing right" than a matter of him loving her as she wanted him to.

Sierra shifted, slid her feet to the floor and stood, thankful for the shadows that wreathed the room beyond the circle of light thrown onto the couch by the lamp atop the table behind it.

"You don't owe me anything, Sam," she told him, her voice a raspy whisper. "This is a situation of my own design. It's not up to you to make it right."

He sat up, swinging his feet off the couch. "That's not how I see it, and I'm doing my best to work this out."

"There's nothing to work out."

"Sierra, we've been all over this. You know my reasoning."

"And I'm telling you that you're wrong in this instance."

He stood. "You don't want me to be an equal partner?"

"That's not what I'm saying. You're already an equal partner."

"In the business, maybe, and if this had stayed just business, we wouldn't be having this conversation."

"Then maybe we should just go back to 'just business' and let it be," she choked out.

He tilted his head. "It's too late for that."

"No," she refuted, shaking her head, but it was.

It was. So when he reached for her, she let herself be drawn into his arms once more.

"Now, listen," he said. "I'm going to work it all out. You'll see. Everything's going to be fine."

Sierra closed her eyes. Sam would always try to fix everything, no matter the cost to himself. God, what had she done to the man she loved? And did she have the strength to undo it?

"I thought I'd take the girls out for dinner, sort of a girls'-night-out thing," Sierra said calmly, putting the finishing touches on the sandwich she was making him. "You're always so tired lately. I figured you could use an evening to yourself."

Sam leaned a hip against the kitchen counter and tilted his head, trying not to feel hurt. "That's what you said last time."

"Well, even with the new guy we hired to help out, you've still been working a lot."

"And you've been avoiding me a lot," he said softly.

She glanced up, and he saw the way her eyes shuttered. "No. I've just tried to be considerate. It's a busy time for you."

"Have I complained?"

"As if you would!"

"Sure, I would, if something wasn't to my liking. I work hard because I want to work hard, Sierra. I'm building something here for all of us."

"I understand that, and I'm grateful for it."

"So why are you cutting me out?"

"I'm not cutting you out. I'm giving you some space."

"For what?"

She stood very still for a long time, looking down at the countertop. Finally she said, "For a life of your own, Sam."

He wasn't sure what she meant by that. "This is my life, Sierra."

"You deserve more than this."

He shook his head. He was on the verge of having everything he wanted, and suddenly she was pulling back. The thought of it stirred in him an emotion that he hadn't felt in a very long time, not since he'd been a helpless kid trying to stand between his brutal father and cowering mother: panic. He hated that feeling. Hated it. And that made him a little angry.

"Are you through with me, Sierra? Is that what this is about? You're through with me?"

She blinked at him. "No! Of course not. How could you even think it? You're such a vital part of our lives now, you and the girls. I—I just…I want you to have all the options you had the day we met."

He didn't get that, but he could see that she was deadly earnest. "Why wouldn't I have?"

She opened her mouth, then closed it again, frowning. "I…we've monopolized so much of your time."

He shrugged. "If I don't mind, I don't know why you should."

She closed her eyes and spoke so softly that he

had to lean forward in order to hear her. "I seduced you, Sam. I seduced you, and I did it on purpose."

Well, that much was true. Smiling, he stepped close and slipped his arms around her.

"Maybe it's time I did the seducing," he whispered on his way to that sweet spot just below her ear. When he fastened his mouth there, she put her head back and moaned softly. He pulled her tighter, letting her feel the bulge growing behind the fly of his jeans. "I think the twins should sleep over tonight, don't you? It's been almost a week."

"Oh, Sam," she said, closing her hands in the fabric of his shirt. "Oh, Sam."

He cupped her face in his hands and kissed her. She trembled against him, but when he raised his head and would have asked her what was *really* wrong, the girls were standing there, grinning at them.

"Ready to go?" Kim asked nonchalantly.

Sam dropped his hands and stepped back, looking at Sierra.

"No," she said. "Sam has to shower and change."

Smiling, he winked at her. "I'll only be a minute."

She reached out to press his hand with her fingers, but before he hurried away, he saw the worry and misery in her eyes. He couldn't for the life of him figure out what that was about—unless she was just concerned about him. He promised himself that he would allay her fears about that soon.

* * *

Sierra sniffed, wiped her eyes, blew her nose and reached for another tissue. She just couldn't seem to stop crying. It was embarrassing. It was frightening. It was dangerous. Anyone could walk in. Anyone could press her for answers. She sniffed again, wiped her eyes again, blew her nose again. And reached for another tissue.

The phone rang, her cell phone. She reached down behind her desk and lifted her purse from the floor, extracting the phone from the side pocket. Her eyes were too bleary to read the message on the tiny screen, so she simply depressed the correct button and put the thing to her ear.

"Hello?"

"Sierra?"

"Sam."

"Are you all right? You sound as if you have a cold."

"Do I? Must be the connection."

"You seem to be getting sick a lot lately. Are you sure you're okay?"

Sierra put her elbow on the desktop, made a fist and rested her forehead against it. "Don't try to take care of me, Sam. Please don't try to take care of me. Not now."

She could feel his confusion in the silence that followed, but she didn't know how to help him with that. Finally, he cleared his throat and said, "I just wanted you to know that the two people you hired today are working out fine. I had my doubts when you sent a middle-aged woman out here, but she's worked rings around the kid. I think he'll do, though. He seems willing to learn.''

Sierra lifted her head and wiped her face. ''That's what I thought, too.''

''Listen, now that we've got some help on board, I'm ready to take a little time for myself. That okay with you?''

She shrugged, realized he couldn't see that and said, ''Sure, Sam, whatever you want.''

''Okay, well, then why don't we drive into Fort Worth for dinner tonight? Just the two of us.''

Sierra sat up straight in her chair. ''Just the two of us?''

''I'll knock off early. Lana will watch the girls. I checked to be sure. What do you say?''

''Just the two of us?'' she asked again, needing to be sure.

''Just you and me, honey.''

Sierra swallowed, feeling her spirits rise. ''That would be wonderful, Sam.''

''It's a date, then.''

A date. Sierra bit her lip to stifle her laughter. A date. After all this time. If that wasn't a classic cart-before-the-horse, she didn't know what was. But she'd take it. Oh, yes, she'd take it.

''I'll be ready and waiting by six.''

''Six it is. See you then''

He broke the connection. Sierra pressed the button that would terminate the call on her end and sat back. They were going on a date. She smiled and hugged herself.

* * *

Sierra sat her fork aside and picked up her glass, sipping the sparkling water. ''That was an excellent dinner.''

''Glad you enjoyed it,'' Sam said. ''How about dessert?''

She waved her hands. ''No way. I'm stuffed.''

''A glass of wine, then. I'm pretty much a beer man myself, but I could go for one more glass of this Chardonnay if you want to join me. It's really good.''

''Thank you, no.''

He leaned forward and urged softly, ''Go ahead. I can afford it.''

Exasperated, Sierra rolled her eyes. ''I never implied that you couldn't. I'm just not much of a drinker.''

A sheepish look overcame him. ''Sorry. I know my pride gets the better of me sometimes. I'll work on it, I promise.''

''Your pride's part of who you are, Sam, and I wouldn't have it any other way.''

He reached across the crisply draped table and covered her hand with his. ''How about naked and in my bed?''

Her heart slammed against the wall of her chest. ''Is that an invitation?''

''Absolutely.''

''Your house?''

''Unless you'd rather go to yours.''

''No.'' This, she knew, was a major step for him.

Was he finally beginning to see that money and possessions didn't matter?

He smiled and signaled the waiter, reaching for his wallet. In short order they were heading for the exit, but as they crossed the now crowded foyer, an unwelcome presence impeded their progress.

"Well, well, fancy meeting you here."

Sierra rocked to a halt, her back bumping against Sam's chest. "Dennis."

Her ex-husband raked them both with a smirk. Sierra noticed that he wore an expensive silk suit and hand-tailored shirt, as opposed to Sam's serviceable sport coat over dark, starched jeans and a gray, finely gauged sweater. He was with a tall, skinny blonde who'd bought herself one cosmetic surgery too many. She had all the perfect features, but they were disproportionate somehow: nose too small, mouth too plump, cheeks too high, eyes too smooth, skin too taut for the shape, length and breadth of her face.

"Treating the boy-toy to a night on the town?"

Sierra felt Sam bristle at her back and lifted a restraining hand. "As a matter of fact," Sierra said, "my partner and I are celebrating the expansion of our business. We recently signed a lucrative contract and hired our first employees."

"But that's something you wouldn't know anything about," Sam put in, "seeing as how your idea of a business deal is pumping your eight-year-old daughter for funds."

"That's a lie!"

"Is it?"

The blonde made herself known then, draping a proprietary arm across Dennis's chest. "Who are these people?" she sniffed, trying to snub them and satisfy her curiosity at the same time.

Sierra smiled wryly. "I'm the lucky one who got away."

"And I'm the one who's gonna rearrange your date's face if he makes that boy-toy crack again," Sam growled.

"You and who else?" Dennis sneered, glancing around as if to remind Sam that they were in a public place.

Sam held up both his fists. "Me and these two."

The blonde's eyes widened, and she drew back as if fearing a blow to her own too-perfect face.

"You better teach some manners to this hayseed," Dennis mocked.

"Or what?" Sam asked mildly, but Dennis only glared. "Yeah, that's what I thought. Come on, honey. We've got celebrating to do."

He shoved open the door, and they found themselves out on the sidewalk, hurrying, arm in arm, toward his big truck.

"So that's the ex," Sam muttered, his hand riding protectively in the small of her back. "I cannot believe the nerve of that guy. No wonder you're so disturbed by Tyree's relationship with him."

"He's still her father," Sierra pointed out, as she had done on too many occasions.

"And always will be," Sam agreed, "but you know what's cheesing him off?"

"That I've got money."

"And that you're my girl now."

Sierra laughed. She felt like a girl again, out on a Friday night with her high school steady, except no teenager had any business indulging in what they were planning. "Come on," she said, and they ran the rest of the way to the truck.

Sam turned on the radio as they drove, and though she could see the speedometer and knew that they were flying low, it was as if they were floating through the night, blood simmering as they anticipated what lay ahead. At one and the same time it seemed as if a mere moment and an eternity passed before the truck rolled up into Sam's narrow, graveled drive. Snagging her hand, he slid out and pulled her out after him. He towed her across the yard and up onto the porch, through the unlocked front door and the darkened house to a small room at the back of the kitchen.

The room was worn but clean, with furnishings consisting of nothing more than a full-sized bed with an old-fashioned metal headboard, a small dresser, side chair, a crate piled with books and a small lamp. The window shades were ancient and yellowed, the faded blue bedspread practically threadbare, but the walls were lined with framed photos of the twins, their mother, the Houstons and a young Sam.

While Sam switched on the stereo in the other room, Sierra fell in love with a photograph of him with a baby tucked into the curve of each arm, grinning hugely. He was thin as a rail and barely looked old enough to shave, but showed strong signs of the man to come. As she stood there staring at that old picture, Sam walked up behind her and placed his hands atop her shoulders.

"You were there when they were born," she whispered.

"Yep. Jonah was in jail for public drunkenness when Mom went into labor, so I was able to come and be with her."

Sierra shook her head and turned into his arms. "I'm so proud of you, Sam. You've overcome so much. You deserve every good thing life has to offer. I'm sorry if I've led you into something you're not comfortable with."

"Now, now," he said, "it's not like that. I'm no kid. I've known what I was doing from the very beginning."

"But you resisted getting involved. I pushed it."

"That's not what made me do it."

"Then what did?"

He grinned. "You're just so darn irresistible."

She smiled at that. "Am I?"

He stepped closer, tightened the arms looped about her waist. "You have to ask?" He bent his head and kissed her, then pulled her against his chest with a sigh. "You've got me jumping through hoops, sweetheart, doing everything I can to make this thing right between us. One day, Sierra, I'll be able to take care of you and Tyree. You've got to believe that."

She pushed back a little, troubled anew. "What if I don't want you to take care of us, Sam?"

He drew away. "You saying you don't want us to be together?"

"No, of course I'm not saying that. I—I'm just not sure what being together means."

"Well, then," he said silkily, moving her toward the bed, "let me show you."

She didn't know how to tell him that sex wasn't enough anymore or how to walk away from the only part of him she might ever have.

Chapter Thirteen

Sam slumped against the steps and watched wearily as Sierra went down on her knees and began tugging at his boots. He shouldn't have eaten before he cleaned up. Now, with his stomach full, his body just wanted to lie down, roll over and pass out.

"You've got to stop this, Sam," Sierra scolded. "You're working too hard. It's ridiculous. I've hired you half a dozen hands, and instead of taking it easier, you try to outwork them all. You're so tired you can't even make it up the stairs to the shower."

"I just need a little rest," he said, knowing that she was right. He had overdone it today, but every row of plants that went into the ground was one more step forward toward his goal, and the way she was looking up at him now with that soft light of concern and admiration in her eyes was enough to make him want to go back out there and put in another few hours. Except it was pitch-black out there now.

She got the second boot off. Dirt trickled out of it and onto her clean floor.

"Oh, I'm sorry, honey," he moaned. "Don't worry. I'll take care of it."

She threw the boot, threw it, literally. Halfway across the foyer. He sat up on the step, gaping at her.

"I am so sick and tired of you taking care of everything!" she yelled. "Is that your only function in life, Sam? Taking care of everyone? Can't anyone take care of you? You talk about being equals, but what's equal about this? I don't give a fig about a little dirt on my floor! It doesn't matter to me anymore whether or not the farm pays off! My only concern is for you and the girls and our—" She broke off and started to cry.

He found the energy to get up off the step and go to her. "Sierra, I'm sorry."

"For what?" she wailed.

He put his arms around her. "I don't really know, to tell you the truth. I guess I'm just too tired to figure it out right now."

She sniffed, calmer now. "It's not your fault, Sam. I don't know what's wrong with me these days."

He sighed. "I think maybe I've left you alone too much with the girls. Tell you what. Tomorrow's

Saturday. We'll take the day. Do nothing. Get some rest.''

"Tomorrow's Sunday, Sam."

"Oh." The days of the past weeks seemed to have run together into one long marathon of planting. "Okay. Same deal."

The room swayed. Sierra caught him with an arm about his waist. "That's it. I'm getting you up those stairs, into a hot shower and to bed, a real bed. No arguments."

He couldn't imagine why he would argue. She turned him toward the stairs, and he draped an arm about her shoulders for support. Together they started up the stairs, one steep step at a time. At the top, she guided him down the hall to her room. She practically hauled him through the bedroom door and slung him onto the side of the bed. He wanted desperately to lie down, but he was too filthy.

"I'm not sure I have the strength to shower."

"I'll help you. My shower has room for two."

Room for two. He liked the sound of that. "I'm afraid I'm just too tired to do you any good, honey. I'm sorry."

"Oh, shut up," she ordered, jerking at his clothes. When she had him stripped down to his pants, she tugged him up and shoved those down. "Step out."

He did. She stepped under his arm and walked him into the bathroom, which was rapidly filling with steam. When had she turned on the shower? he wondered. He seemed to have lost some time. She opened the wide glass door and shoved him

through it. The hot sting of the water was pure
heaven, but it made his knees even weaker than
they were. He leaned against the glass brick and let
the spray pummel him.

The door opened again, and Sierra stepped inside, gloriously naked. "Mmm," he said and got
his hands on her, but she twisted away and fiddled
with the water temperature, then turned back, a bottle of body wash and cloth in hand. He chuckled as
she began to scrub the dirt off him. So she wanted
to take care of him, did she? He stood there and let
her, and soon the weariness ebbed somewhat. By
the time she got to shampooing his hair, he was
hard as stone. Shaking away her hands, he stuck his
head beneath the strongest part of the spray and
rinsed out the lather, then he shoved her up into the
corner and began kissing her.

She put her head back when he lifted her legs
around his waist and pushed himself up into her.
"I thought you were too tired."

"I guess I'm never too tired for you, honey," he
said, fixing his mouth to hers.

She put her arms around his neck, and his body
did what it knew instinctively to do, but he was too
tired, and within moments he exploded inside her.
After that, he was almost too weak to stand, but as
he slumped, she put her feet to the floor once more
and pushed him back against the opposite wall.
Quickly, she shut off the water and went out, re-
turning moments later with towels. He took one
from her and lethargically rubbed his head and
chest before trusting himself to step out of the

shower stall and into the bathroom. She took over then, briskly toweling him dry. When she was done with him, she started on herself, ordering, "Get in the bed."

He didn't argue, just dragged himself into the other room. She had turned down the covers, so he lifted them and got inside. "Ahhhhhh."

She showed up just as his eyes were drifting shut, wrapped head to knees in toweling. She bent and pressed her mouth to his.

"Where'r m'girs?" he asked against her lips.

"Downstairs cleaning up after dinner. Now go to sleep."

"S'erra?"

"Hmm?"

He meant to say that he loved her, that it was all for her, for them, that he was going to let her take care of him a little more often, that this was the pinnacle of his life, finding her, loving her, being loved by her, but the words drifted away with consciousness.

Sierra dressed in the same clothes she was wearing when Sam had come in and quickly dried her hair before going back downstairs. The girls were in the den watching television, the twins on the couch, Tyree sprawled in a chair.

"Is Sam okay?" Keli asked.

"Sam's sleeping. He's worn-out."

"No one works as hard as Sam," Tyree said, a touch of pride in her voice.

"You're right about that." She sat down on the sofa next to the twins.

"Where's Sam sleeping?" Kim wanted to know.

Sierra looked determinedly at the television screen. "In my bed. You and Keli will have to sleep in the guest room tonight."

"Okay."

"Where will you sleep, Mom?" Tyree asked idly.

Sierra thought of all the nights that Sam had spent here on this couch. "Here," she said.

"You could sleep with Sam," Keli commented. "It's a big bed."

"There's room," Tyree agreed.

Sierra just smiled warily and said, "Listen, Sam needs to sleep in tomorrow, so when you get up be real quiet about it, okay, just in case."

"Could we stay up late?" Tyree asked hopefully.

"Yeah, then we won't get up too early," Kim added.

Sierra chuckled. "Okay. We'll make a slumber party of it."

"Oh, boy," Keli said. "Popcorn!"

"Well, of course. Popcorn is a slumber party requirement."

"And sodas," Tyree insisted. "Please, Mom."

"Yeah! Please, Mom," Kim echoed.

Sierra's breath caught. Was Kim really starting to think of her as her mother? If so, she'd better act like one.

"We'll split a couple," Sierra decreed flatly. "And after that it's fruit juice or water."

"Yippee!" Keli exclaimed. Launching up, she threw her arms around Sierra's neck and smacked a happy kiss on her cheek. Tyree just grinned.

"Let's see what's on TV later," Kim suggested eagerly, and Sierra got up to make popcorn and divide two sodas four ways.

Sierra closed the bedroom door and went to the linen closet at the end of the hall to pull out the usual blanket and sheet. She'd take a pillow from her own bed. The girls had made it, surprisingly, to just past midnight before yawns and droopy eyelids had spurred Sierra to herd them upstairs and tuck them in. Now, carrying the linens, she walked to her own room and slipped through the door.

Sam lay just as she'd left him, on his back, one hand resting palm up on the pillow next to his head, the other palm down on his chest. He looked about eighteen, but she well knew the strong, virile man inside that sleeping facade. She had never known a man as determined, as hardworking, as true to his principles, as caring as Samuel Jayce. In many ways, she felt unworthy of him. Yet, she knew, with some sadness, that he was hers for the taking. Sam's overdeveloped sense of responsibility would hand him to her on a silver platter, but she didn't want him that way, and Sam deserved more than another set of responsibilities.

After placing the bedding on a chair, she pulled her nightshirt from the dresser drawer, using the light from the hallway by which to navigate, and went into the bathroom to brush her teeth and change. Ready for sleep, she padded out on bare feet to retrieve her bedding and head downstairs, but instead of going all the way around the big bed for the pillow, she just reached across Sam for it. He sat bolt upright, nearly scaring the life out of her.

"What's wrong?" he asked, blinking.

"Nothing. Go back to sleep."

He looked around the darkened room. "The girls?"

"Sleeping. Lie down. Everything's fine." She urged him back with a hand on his chest.

He sighed and closed his eyes, more asleep than awake. "Come back to bed then," he mumbled.

Back to bed? "I'm going to sleep on the couch," she said softly.

He rolled onto his side and limply patted the spot next to him. "C'mon."

Did he know what he was saying? Probably not. On the other hand, what could it hurt? The girls themselves had suggested that they share. Of course, the girls had no idea what sharing a bed could mean for a man and a woman. But not tonight. It was late, and they both needed sleep. The girls would sleep late, probably nine at least. Besides, she wanted this night beside him, even if it was only to sleep. She set the alarm for eight and went to shut the door. She didn't even think of locking it. Instead, she made her way around the bed and slipped beneath the covers.

"Sure, honey," Sam mumbled, and rolled toward her, winding up facedown with his shoulder over hers and his arm across her waist.

Sierra smiled. He was obviously dreaming. She chose to believe he was dreaming about her. Hugging that thought tight, she closed her eyes and slept.

At some point she heard a short, sharp bleat, then a faint thump. The bed rocked slightly, and she remembered thinking that she probably ought to get up. The next thing she knew an oddly familiar but out-of-place voice jolted her awake.

"Good God! I should have known."

She blinked, realized it was daylight and frowned at the dream that had awakened her, unable to recall anything but the sound of her father's voice. Then she turned her head and finally understood that it was no dream. Her father towered over her bed, his face like thunder. To make matters worse, Sam suddenly sat up.

"Huh? What?"

Frank McAfree pointed an accusing finger at him but clearly addressed Sierra. "Who the hell is this? I knew something was wrong when Tyree said you were having a 'sleep-in'!"

"Daddy," Sierra said, pushing hair out of her face.

Sam gaped at her, then glanced around the room. When his gaze reached Frank, he started to get out of the bed.

"Don't." Sierra laid a restraining hand on his forearm, and he glanced down at himself, obviously realized that he was naked and immediately subsided.

"What's going on?" he croaked, glowering.

"I came to check on my daughter!" Frank practically roared. "And I find her in bed with a man—and Tyree in the house!"

Sam turned a wide, accusing glare on Sierra. Moaning, she sat up. What a way to start a morning! She wanted to pull the covers up over her head and pretend it hadn't happened, but Frank was sputtering outrage all over them even now.

"How old are you? My God, don't you have any decency? I never thought this of you, Sierra."

"Will you just go downstairs now? I'll be down in a minute," she said miserably.

"*We'll* be down in a minute," Sam corrected.

Sierra gulped. Frank made a disgusted sound and stomped out of the room. Sierra dropped her head into her hands. Sam leaped out of bed and began looking around for his clothes.

"What the hell is going on? Is that your *father?*"

"Yes. Your clothes are in the dressing room," Sierra informed him. "Dad obviously dropped by, and something Tyree said made him come up here."

Sam was already striding angrily for the dressing room. Resigned, Sierra got up and pulled on the same clothes she'd already put on twice now. She was barely decent when Sam strode back in again, yanking on a T-shirt over his jeans.

"I think I know how we wound up in bed together," he said brusquely, "but you'd better tell me just the same."

"You were so tired," she began. "I couldn't let you drive home, and I didn't want you sleeping on the couch. This just seemed the best place for you." She gestured toward the bed. "The girls actually suggested that we share. Because the bed is so big." She glanced at the folded linens on the chair. "I was going to sleep on the couch, but then you sort of woke up and said…" She bit her lip.

He sighed. "I knew I was in your bed. I think I was dreaming that we were there together."

She bowed her head. "I knew that. I shouldn't have lain down with you. I thought that if I set the alarm I could get up before anyone else." As she said that she looked at the alarm, frowning.

Sam put a hand to the back of his neck and admitted sheepishly, "I, uh, think I turned it off. I must've thought it was mine. I remember hearing it, but I guess I thought I set it by mistake. I seemed to recall promising you that we'd sleep in."

"But we weren't supposed to sleep in together," she added.

Sam sighed. "So naturally your father *would* walk in on us."

Sierra hung her head. "I'm sorry, Sam."

Sam nodded, then rubbed a hand over his face. "I guess we should go down now."

"Maybe you should let me handle this, Sam," she suggested wanly.

The look he gave her said that he thought she'd handled enough already and not exactly with sterling results. Unfortunately, she couldn't disagree. He walked to the door, opened it and lifted an arm toward her. It had all the authority of an order. Sierra reluctantly trudged out onto the landing and down the stairs.

Frank paced the living room. He was wearing golf clothes as if he'd come straight from an early game on links.

"This is my father, Frank McAfree," Sierra said as they entered the room.

Sam walked right up to him and put out his hand. "Sam Jayce. I'm Sierra's partner."

Frank ignored the hand that Sam offered him and glared at Sierra. "This is the kid you were telling me about?"

"He's not a kid," Sierra defended quietly, watching a muscle flex in Sam's jaw. He parked that rejected hand at his hip and squared his shoulders, widening his stance slightly.

"Maybe you'd like a tour of the farm," Sam suggested firmly, "to check out the operation."

"Maybe," Frank growled, "but first I want an explanation. What the hell did you two think you were doing?"

"Sleeping," Sierra said. "Just sleeping."

"Don't tell me you're not lovers!"

"We are," Sam confirmed easily. "For now." Sierra blinked and lifted a hand to her chest. It felt as if someone had poked her there—hard—with a finger. He might as well have said, "Temporarily." Sierra swallowed. "But we don't generally spend the night together, not with the girls in the house."

"Girls?" Frank echoed, looking at Sam. "You have a daughter, too?"

"He's raising his twin sisters," Sierra said quickly. "I guess they're still asleep upstairs. We stayed up late, the girls and I. Sam worked hard yesterday. He was too tired to drive home. I had to literally put him to bed, and later I just...I didn't see the point in making a bed on the couch. I—I thought I'd be up before anyone else," she finished lamely.

Frank pointed a finger at the wall, hissing, "Your daughter is in there eating cereal. Don't you think she knows that you were upstairs sleeping with him? She told me herself. 'Mommy and Sam are having a sleep-in.'"

"She only meant that we were sleeping late. I told the girls last night that I wanted Sam to sleep in because he needed the rest. That's all that means."

Frank was shaking his head. "This is irresponsible. Even for you, Sierra."

"Now hold on there," Sam interjected. "Sierra is not irresponsible. Okay, I agree that we shouldn't have been in the bed together. And we never have been before, not with the girls in the house. You have my word on that. But Sierra is not irresponsible."

"Oh, no? What do you call this place?"

"All right," Sam conceded with a nod of the head, "maybe the house is a little much, but to Sierra security means a real home. You ought to know that. So maybe she should've financed part of it, scaled back a bit. Everybody makes mistakes. Besides, it's worked out fine. The business is in good shape. We're going to turn a profit, a substantial profit, and she's going to recoup her investment here in spades.''

"And you're making sure none of it gets away from you, aren't you, buster,'' Frank accused.

"That's not fair, Daddy,'' Sierra said sharply, leaping to Sam's defense. "Sam has worked as hard as three men at this. Why do you think he was too exhausted to drive himself home last night? We've borrowed money on Sam's credit and reputation. The farm was my idea, but it's his accomplishment. He's the one making it happen. He doesn't have to romance me to see his share of the profits.''

"And for the record, I resent the implication that I would,'' Sam added flatly.

Frank looked at Sam, shrewdly assessing, and Sam stared back unflinchingly. Finally, Frank looked away. Sam turned to Sierra.

"Why don't you start some breakfast, honey? I'm going to show your father around the place now. Set an extra plate.''

"I won't be staying,'' Frank said gruffly. "I've eaten already.''

Sam shrugged. "Suit yourself. I still think you ought to see the operation.''

Frank nodded sharply, just once.

Sierra licked her lips, wondering if she dared let these two out of her sight, but then Sam smiled and kissed the top of her head, while Frank cleared his throat and looked away. She decided that she could trust Sam to handle this. Maybe if Frank saw what the farm was becoming, he would at least understand that she had made a wise choice in Sam as a business partner.

She turned and walked out of the room.

Sam took Frank McAfree out the front. He was boiling mad, but he was determined to be respectful, too, mindful of the man with whom he was dealing. He made sure the door was closed firmly behind them before confronting the older man.

"Now, then," he began tautly, facing Frank. "Number one, don't ever walk into Sierra's bedroom uninvited again. She's not a child. She's entitled to privacy, especially in her own house. Number two, you're Sierra's father, and I understand your concern, so I'm willing to suck up whatever you throw down on me, but don't you ever speak to her like that again. Sierra doesn't deserve to be called irresponsible. I don't care what mistakes she may have made in the past, she doesn't deserve that attitude you turned on her."

"Doesn't she?" Frank asked, lifting an eyebrow.

"Do you think I'd trust my girls to her if she was irresponsible? Do you think I'd have gone into business with her? Do you think I'd let myself fall in love with her?"

Frank narrowed his eyes. "How old are you?"

Sam threw up his hands, brought them back to his hips, dropped his head and tapped a foot impatiently, doing his best to tamp down his temper. "What does that have to do with anything?"

"I don't know," Frank said. "Maybe nothing."

Mollified a bit, Sam folded his arms. "In that case, I'm twenty-four."

Frank snorted. "I didn't know my butt from a hole in the ground at twenty-four."

"Well, I do."

Frank looked away. Sam could've sworn he was grinning, but when he looked back, his visage was stern. "We'll see about that."

"We sure will," Sam agreed.

"Let's get on with that tour."

Sam turned. "This way." He led Frank toward the greenhouse, figuring he might as well start at the beginning. "And keep up," he grumbled when Frank seemed to hang back a step. "We've got a lot of ground to cover by the time my breakfast is ready."

Sam didn't see the quick grin that flashed across Frank McAfree's face, nor would he see it again or hear a word of praise before the fellow climbed into his big, luxury sedan almost an hour later and drove away.

Chapter Fourteen

"What happened?" Sierra asked once the girls were safely out of earshot. She folded the dish towel and laid it aside, turning to face Sam.

"Not much," Sam answered, leaning a hip against the counter. "I showed him around. He left."

"I'm sorry, Sam. This is all my fault."

Sam shrugged. "He doesn't have any business coming into your bedroom that way, even if he is your father, and he really doesn't have any business talking to you like you're a wayward teenager, either, and I told him so."

"Oh, Sam, you didn't."

"I darn well did."

She sighed. "What did he say?"

"About all he said of any importance was to tell Tyree he'd see her at her birthday party next week."

"Apparently he came by to ask her what she wanted for a present and see if he could do anything to help with the party," Sierra revealed.

"Good," Sam said. "That's what grandfathers are supposed to do."

"You didn't argue then?" she asked weakly.

"No, we didn't argue," Sam said, reaching for her. She came into his arms feeling as foolish and irresponsible as her father thought her to be.

"I am sorry, Sam. I shouldn't have gotten into that bed with you."

"Best night's sleep I've had in a long, long time," he said dismissively. "Problem is, it's going to be awful tough now to crawl alone into that lumpy thing back at my place."

"I wish you didn't have to," Sierra whispered, holding on to him.

"Me, too," he said, but he didn't suggest that it could change, and she didn't dare suggest it herself.

Sierra spent a busy week getting ready for Tyree's ninth birthday. Sam and the girls helped, especially Sam, who convinced Sierra to take back all but one of the gifts she'd bought and keep the plans simple. Sierra felt strongly about not excluding anyone in Tyree's class at school, however, so the guest list included some twenty-six children, including the twins. They invited several adults as well, all people close to Tyree, and enlisted Gwyn to bake the cake and make some sandwiches. In addition, Gwyn's two teenage children would be coming along, and they had planned games to play with the children.

Sierra cleaned the house, stocked ice cream and the ingredients for punch, bought party favors and, the morning of the party, decked the place with decorations, including a big banner that stretched all the way across the dining room. Tyree and the twins were so excited they could barely contain themselves. Sam came in from the field at lunch-time, cleaned up and helped Sierra set out chips and nuts and dainty paper plates and matching napkins printed with the chosen theme. They stacked the birthday gifts in the living room, including the one that Sam and the twins had brought.

Gwyn and her kids, sixteen-year-old Molly and thirteen-year-old Chip arrived first. The girls squealed with delight over the birthday cake and ran off to place another gift on the pile. Gwyn smiled at Sam.

"Hello, Sam. It's good to see you again."

"Ms. Dunstan, Molly, Chip. How've ya'll been?"

"Hanging in there," Gwyn said. "Sierra's told me you've been working hard." That wasn't all Sierra had told her, but thankfully Gwyn didn't allude to that.

"It's coming together real fine," Sam said. Then he turned to Sierra. "Honey, you want me to bring in that punch bowl now?"

Gwyn raised her eyebrows, and Molly looked

quickly between Sam and Sierra. "That would be fine, thanks," Sierra answered mildly. Sam went off, and Gwyn sent Molly and Chip to look after the girls.

"He doesn't seem like a reluctant lover to me," Gwyn murmured, sidling up to Sierra.

"Maybe not so reluctant now," Sierra answered softly, "but…"

"You're in love with him," Gwyn said.

Sierra closed her eyes. "And how."

"Are you afraid it's not mutual?" Gwyn asked.

"I seduced him," Sierra reminded her, nodding.

"It's just sex for him then. That's what you're saying?"

"Not exactly," Sierra whispered miserably.

"Not a bit of it, I'd say," Gwyn murmured. The doorbell rang then, and Sierra hurried off to answer it, without a chance to explain to Gwyn that she had somehow become another responsibility to Sam, who collected responsibilities like most men collected sports memorabilia.

After that, Sierra barely had a moment to think, let alone carry on personal discussions. Everyone seemed to arrive at once. Her father led the way, followed almost immediately by her friend and fellow heiress, Valerie Blunt Keene, Val's husband Ian, the town fire marshal, and her mother Delores. Always the trendsetter, Val wore a denim mini, thigh-high boots and a huge sweater with sleeves that hung down to her fingertips. Her highlighted blond hair was twisted up into a spiky topknot that only a hairdresser, which she was, could manage.

Ian, who was tall, dark and movie-star handsome, constantly looked at his wife as if he could be overcome by temptation and take a bite out of her any moment.

Dennis showed up next, edgy but alone, and in the midst of a wave of kids. A steady stream of cars dropped off children for the next half hour. Avis Lorimer, the last of the heiresses, arrived in the middle of it, looking beautiful, as usual, with her long, chocolate-brown hair waving about her oval face. She wore an expensive knit pantsuit of the same dark blue shade as her exotic eyes. Surprisingly, she was accompanied by a pale, silent, smirky, younger man whom she introduced as her stepson.

Sierra welcomed Ellis Lorimer graciously, wondering why he'd want to impose himself on a child's birthday party. She sensed that something odd was going on, but one more guest was no burden, and she didn't have time to ponder the situation.

With the help of Molly, Chip and Sam, Sierra oversaw several games for the kids, handed out party favors and tried to make sure that the adults all had food and drink. When it came time to open presents, Sierra was very glad that she had listened to Sam. The pile was obscene. Even Tyree seemed overwhelmed and a little embarrassed. She came to Sierra with a proposal.

"Mom," she whispered, "maybe I ought to just open the ones from the kids. Save the rest for later."

Sierra dropped an arm around her. "I think that's a great idea."

"And maybe," Tyree went on, "I could share with Kim and Keli. Just the kids' gifts, though."

Sierra could've kissed her, but she knew too well how that would be received there in front of all her friends. "We'll have to ask Sam about that."

"Could we?"

"You get started, and I'll ask Sam what he thinks."

Next year, Sierra thought, they would stipulate no presents, at least not from the kids. In the past, Tyree had celebrated her birthday with one or two close friends, her mom and her grandfather. Sierra had longed to give her the kind of big, loud party that seemed the norm. She realized now that they hadn't quite gotten it right.

Tyree began the unwrapping with more tact than Sierra had expected. She displayed a kind of understated excitement and pleasure that frankly made Sierra proud. While Frank was busy snapping photos, Sierra made her way over to Sam, who stood in one corner with most of the other adults.

"Can I talk to you a minute?"

"Sure, honey. What's up?"

She pulled him a little away from the others. He looped an arm about her neck and bent his head to hers as she explained Tyree's proposal.

Sam glanced over his shoulder at Tyree, smiled down at Sierra and winked. "I told you that girl was okay." Impulsively, she hugged him. His arm about her, he half turned to watch Tyree. When

Tyree looked his way, he smiled and nodded. Tyree seemed to sit a little taller, smile a little brighter. Sierra unobtrusively set aside the gifts brought by the adults, a half dozen or so, and whispered an explanation to that group.

Cutting the cake was the most fun part of the day for Sierra. Tyree blew out the candles on the first try, then passed out pieces while Gwyn and Molly cut. Sierra and Delores dished out ice cream and Avis and Val filled punch cups. Sam made himself useful mopping up spills, of which there were several. Sierra proudly divulged Tyree's plan for splitting up the gifts, and Delores suggested that another remedy for such largesse might be to donate several of the still-packaged toys to a local church that collected them throughout the year in order to provide Christmas gifts for underprivileged children.

"I'll mention that to the girls," Sierra decided, sure they would want to donate. "And next year we won't let this happen."

Thankfully, the afternoon wore to a close, and their young guests began to depart as the appointed end of the party arrived. When the last little one had gone off, the adults once more gathered in the living room for the final gift opening. When Sierra told Tyree about Delores's suggestion, she quickly, brightly agreed.

"We got some just alike anyway," Kim announced.

We. Sierra shared a smile with Sam. Apparently Tyree had informed the twins of the plan. Kim and

Keli began separating out the gifts that would go to the church while Tyree opened the remainder.

She thanked and hugged her grandfather for the new video game he'd bought, then did the same with Val and Ian, Delores, Gwyn and her kids and Avis. When the pile of gifts was gone, Sam and Dennis, very conspicuously, were the only ones who hadn't received a hug. Tyree had opened a gift from the twins earlier, so Sam was off the hook, but she glanced at her father uncertainly.

Dennis spread his hands, ducked his head and said quite unabashedly, "I'm sorry, pumpkin, but you know how it is with me. I'm not made out of money like your mother is."

Sierra could've choked him, but she put the best possible face on it. "That's okay. She got so much stuff that she's giving most of it away and still has lots left, don't you, sweetie?"

Tyree smiled thinly. "Uh-huh."

"The most important thing is that your dad was here to help you celebrate," Sierra went on, and Tyree nodded vigorously.

Sam stepped forward then, one hand behind his back. "Maybe," he said, "just one more gift, a real personal one." He brought his hand around and offered a flat, rectangular package that was obviously a book.

Tyree tore off the ribbon and paper, smiled widely and held up the gift. "It's all about flowers!"

Sam went down on his haunches in front of her. "It sure is, cupcake. Flowers are our legacy. Maybe someday what your mom and I are building here will go to you and the twins, in which case, you ought to know something about it, don't you think?''

Tyree nodded, put the book down on the armchair beside her and reached out with both arms. ''Thank you, Sam.''

''Well, isn't that just grand,'' Dennis said snidely. He pointed a finger at Sierra. ''This is on you. That's the son of a murderer you brought in here to charm my little girl. Is that the kind of influence you want our kid to have?''

Sam released Tyree and rose to his full height, turning on Dennis. ''Watch your mouth,'' he said softly.

Dennis ignored him, addressing Frank instead. ''Did you know that this *boy* is the son of a murderer?''

The room fell into a deadly silence, then Sam looked to Delores and asked quietly, ''Would you mind helping the girls take the gifts upstairs?''

''Why don't you two help her?'' Gwyn said to her teenagers as Delores nodded and moved forward.

''Well, well,'' Ellis Lorimer murmured, ''interesting.''

Avis shot him a killing look and said, ''I think we ought to be going.''

''No, no, that's all right,'' Sam said, waving a hand at her as Delores hustled the girls out of the room and the teenagers followed. ''Dennis has thoughtfully pointed out that I'm the son of a murderer. No denying it. He's absolutely right. It's common knowledge around here. Now I want to go on record with this. My old man is scum. It's an ugly fact of my life. And the crap you've just pulled here, Carlton, is just like something he would do.''

Dennis dropped his jaw. ''Why, you sniveling little—''

''And one more thing,'' Sam went on hotly, stepping forward. ''I was man enough at fourteen to stomp my old man into a greasy spot on the ground, and I can sure do the same with the likes of you now.''

''Are you threatening me?'' Dennis demanded.

''You got it, genius. Bring up that ugliness again in front of my girls and I'll be throwing a rug over the stain you'll leave on the floor.''

''What's wrong with right now, hotshot?''

''Not a thing,'' Sam said, surging forward.

Sierra quickly stepped between them. ''That's enough.''

''Get out of my way, Sierra. The jerk's got it coming after what he said the other night and now.''

''Hoo-hoo,'' Dennis crowed, ''the boy-toy is throwing a fit.''

''I mean it, Sierra,'' Sam ground out, his hands balled into fists. The veins in his neck were standing out.

''I'm not going to let you fight.''

''You're not my mother!'' Sam bawled.

''That's right. I'm your partner and lover!'' she shouted back. ''Now calm down.''

"Yeah, Sammy boy, calm down," Dennis jeered.

Val grabbed her husband by the wrist then, saying, "Ian, this is getting out hand. Can't you stop it?"

"Oh, I think Sam's doing just fine," Ian drawled. "If it was me, I'd already have decked the bum."

Suddenly everyone was shouting—with Dennis egging on Sam, Sierra scolding them both, Frank demanding to know why no one had told him about Sam's background and everyone else trying to calm the situation. Sierra finally got the floor by stamping her foot and screaming, "Stop it! Stop it!"

An uneasy silence descended. Sierra caught a breath and looked at her father. "You want to know about Sam's background? All right, I'll tell you about Sam's background. He left home at fourteen because his mother was afraid he was going to step between her and her husband one too many times. When his father started menacing his foster family, Sam left them, too, to keep them safe. He put himself through college after that, and when his father finally murdered his mother, Sam took over raising his two baby sisters.

"By working harder than any other three men I know, Sam established himself as a custom farmer and built a sterling reputation as a businessman and parent. All that at twenty-four. And if that wasn't enough, he took me on as a partner. He saw in me and my plans what no one else did, and almost singlehandedly he's made those dreams a reality. S & S Farms is going to be a success, a huge success, and Sam's not just the brawn behind that, he's the brains, too. I wanted to prove to you what a savvy businesswoman I could be, Daddy, but the truth is that without Sam I'm just a florist with a big bank account I didn't earn.''

''That's what he's in it for!'' Dennis exclaimed. ''He's after your money!''

Sam stepped around Sierra and aimed a fist at Dennis Carlton's chin in the same powerful, fluid movement. Dennis went down like a brick wall behind a wrecking ball. A communal gasp went up, and for a moment everyone froze. Then Ian casually walked over and glanced down at Dennis.

''Out cold.'' He looked up and clapped Sam on the shoulder. ''Good work. I'd have torn the head off any man who made that remark to or about me. Fact is, I had Val put her money into trust and insisted on a prenup just so no one could say I married her for her money.''

''Is that right?'' Sam said, his hands on his hips.

''That's a fact,'' Ian confirmed. Dennis moaned and rolled his head. Ian crooked a finger at Ellis Lorimer then, saying, ''Come on. We'll help you take out the garbage.''

''Make sure he's all right before you let him drive away from here,'' Gwyn admonished as the three men hauled Dennis up onto his feet. He grumbled and shook his head, but he didn't struggle as the three men bundled him out into the entry and through the front door, presumably to his car.

''I always said that man was a sorry one,'' Frank commented.

"I hope you're not talking about Sam," Sierra snapped.

"Sam?" Frank said. "I was talking about Dennis. Sam, now there's a man." He nodded emphatically. "You were right about him, and I'm not above saying I was wrong. You chose well this time, Sierra. You chose well. Now I think I'll go say goodbye to my granddaughter."

Sierra stood there with her mouth open as he left the room. Val and Gwyn both looked at her and began to laugh behind their hands. Avis just smiled. Sierra shook her head. She was feeling a little giddy now that all the excitement had died down.

"Some birthday party," she muttered.

"It's been interesting, you've gotta say that," Gwyn cracked.

"The kids had a good time," Avis pointed out helpfully.

"I kind of think the highlight was seeing Dennis lying there like a stone," Val added with a grin.

Sierra giggled, remembering the instant before Sam's fist had connected with Dennis's chin. The look of surprise on Dennis's face was imbedded in her brain—surprise and crossed eyes. "He must have a glass jaw."

"Out like a light," Valerie confirmed, snickering.

"The bigger they talk, the harder they fall," Avis quipped.

They all laughed. Sierra got a hold on herself first. "Okay, okay. This is supposed to be a celebration, but I don't want Tyree to catch us laughing at her dad.''

Avis immediately sobered, Gwyn cleared her throat and Val straightened, nodding. "Speaking of celebrations," Val said, rocking back on her heels. "I have some good news."

"Oh, yeah?" Gwyn said. "What's that smug look about then?"

Valerie smiled broadly. "I'm pregnant."

Gwyn squealed like a schoolgirl, and suddenly they were all laughing again and hugging like they hadn't seen each other in decades.

"I'm going to have a baby!" Valerie exclaimed happily, as if she couldn't quite believe it yet herself.

"Me, too!" Sierra blurted, still laughing. The next instant she realized what she'd said and clapped a hand over her mouth, but that cat was already out of the bag and tearing around the house, clawing everything in its path. Sierra looked at the three pairs of eyes staring at her, then realized that only two of them were actually fixed on her. The third set, Gwyn's, was looking right past her to the doorway. Sierra whirled around.

There stood Ian and Ellis Lorimer. And Sam.

He looked like Dennis had when they'd hauled him up off the floor.

Horrified, Sierra felt the bottom drop out of her world.

Chapter Fifteen

"This is wonderful!" Gwyn exclaimed. "This is better than the inheritance!"

Ian walked across the floor and slipped his arms around his wife, a faint, secretive smile curling one corner of his mouth. Sam just stood there, expressionless.

"Oh, I'm so happy for you all," Avis said quietly, hugging first Val and then Sierra.

Val beamed. Sierra managed to jerk her gaze away from Sam and almost smile, but inside she was quaking.

"When?" Gwyn insisted on knowing. She looked first to Valerie.

"Five months, two weeks and four days more,"

Val answered, rubbing her slightly rounded tummy through the big sweater.

"You hope," Gwyn told her. "Molly was eleven days late. It felt like eleven months."

Valerie made a face. "I don't want him to be late. I can hardly stand the anticipation now."

"Him?" Gwyn echoed.

"We won't know for a couple weeks," Ian said patiently. "That's when they do the sonogram."

"It's a boy," Valerie insisted. "I know it is."

"Then it must be a boy!" Gwyn exclaimed, hugging them both. After flashing a lightning-quick glance at Sam, who still just stood there in the doorway, she turned to Sierra with a raised eyebrow.

Sierra shook her head and whispered, "I don't know yet." She felt sick to her stomach, sick at heart, just sick.

"Well, this really does call for celebration," Avis announced in that sultry voice of hers. "I propose a toast. Shall we adjourn to the punch bowl?"

"Absolutely," Gwyn agreed, linking her arm with Sierra's and bodily turning her toward the dining room. Avis hurried ahead. Val and Ian followed Gwyn, who was pulling Sierra along. Ellis glanced at Sam, slid his hands into his pockets and strolled after them.

Avis began passing out cups. Gwyn picked up two and pushed them both into Sierra's hands with a slight jerk of her head toward the living room. Sierra sucked in air and steeled herself. She had to face Sam sooner or later, might as well be sooner. She wished to God that she hadn't blurted it out like that. He shouldn't have found out this way that he was going to be a father. She hadn't intended that he find out at all unless, by some miracle, he declared his undying love in the next few weeks.

How she would have kept it from him was something she hadn't worked out yet, but she'd been toying with the idea of whisking away with Tyree on a tour of Europe, or some such thing, then selling her share of the farm and simply not coming back. She really hadn't thought it through yet. Her mind just wouldn't seem to wrap around the problem. Now she had a whole new set of problems.

Oh, God, what had she done to her Sam? How could she make him understand what had happened?

The words *I'm sorry* were weighing on her tongue even as she turned back toward the living room, but when she looked to the doorway, it was empty. She moved on into the room, scanning it rapidly, before plunking the punch cups down onto a sofa table and rushing out into the entry.

No Sam.

She all but bounded up the stairs, punishing herself. Breathing hard, she ran from room to room, knowing even as she did so that Sam had gone.

Sam felt as if he'd been poleaxed.

He kept hearing, over and over again, Valerie Keene say that she was going to have a baby and Sierra laughingly exclaim, "Me, too!"

Whether conversation went on after that or not, he couldn't have said. His ears felt dead to any words other than those. He watched everyone else embracing, laughing, talking, but it seemed unreal, like something playing across a movie screen, something apart from him.

"I'm going to have a baby!"

"Me, too!"

Everyone began walking away. He didn't even think about following. It just didn't seem a possibility, didn't seem anything to do with him.

"I'm going to have a baby!"

"Me, too!"

He had to think about that, but not here. He couldn't think here, so he turned around and walked out. He moved toward the fields out of pure habit, but when he saw his truck, he just got in it and started it up. He didn't even realize that he was going back to his place until he found himself turning into his own driveway.

Stomping the brake, he brought the truck to a halt and shut off the engine. He sat there staring through the windshield at the small, weary frame house where he had grown up, and it occurred to him suddenly that it and forty bare acres were all he really had to show for all his hard work. Then he frowned.

No, that wasn't true. He owned a quarter-million dollars' worth of equipment, mostly paid for, and a partnership in a potentially lucrative business. He owned half of every plant in the ground back at the farm and all those still to be set out. He had half of two greenhouses, one not quite finished yet, and a bright, secure future—as secure as anyone's, anyway. But that wasn't all.

He had Kim and Keli. He had Tyree. He had a baby on the way. His chest swelled, and his head felt light. Leaning forward, he gripped the steering wheel hard, feeling it bite into his hands, and for a moment he couldn't breathe, couldn't reason. And then a whole thought sprang into his mind. He hoped it was a girl.

He heaved out a breath. He seemed to do pretty well with the female of the species. Another girl. Aw, God, a pretty little redhead with her mother's smile and temper and his…heart. That little girl already had his heart. Although a boy wouldn't be bad, either. He'd teach his son to be strong and hardworking and determined, but gentle and thoughtful, too. He saw freckles and a red head, a stubborn chin, an impish gleam in round eyes that shined with pride.

A dampening truth followed. He'd have to tell any child about his or her grandfather, what he'd done to their grandmother. But there was Frank, too. Sam thought of how Frank had snapped photos of Tyree at her birthday party, how he'd wanted to protect her, even from her own mom, if necessary. He might be overbearing, even high-handed, but he would be a good grandfather.

Finally Sam faced something that had hovered behind everything else. Sierra. How he felt about her, about her being pregnant, about learning of it for the first time by accident with a room full of people. He knew that he ought to be angry, and on some level he was. She should've told him as soon as she'd even suspected that she could be pregnant. Maybe she'd even gotten pregnant on purpose; he couldn't absolutely rule out the possibility.

Yes, he had plenty of reason to be angry, but he couldn't quite manage it. That little spark of indignation, of embarrassment, of misgiving lay buried beneath an overwhelming layer of inevitability and a warm, comfortable blanket of deep, abiding emotion.

They'd have to live at the farm, of course. No way this house could accommodate them all. Even Sierra's house wouldn't be the best fit, however. He imagined the girls would like to at least have adjoining bedrooms, and they needed a nursery. Couldn't forget the nursery. They were going to have to do some remodeling, a little wall moving, door opening. The study could move downstairs. What did they need with both a den and a living room, anyway?

He was glad Sierra had built that big old house now, even if his pride did feel a little pricked that she would be providing their home. He was darn sure going to follow Ian's advice about that prenuptial agreement. All in all, however, Sam was a man satisfied, if a little stunned, with the way his life was turning out.

He got of the truck and headed for the garage, where he picked up some empty boxes before going on into the house.

* * *

"Don't worry. Take all the time you need," Gwyn told her.

Sierra nodded, barely keeping the tears at bay, and rolled up the window of her car. She hadn't needed to tell Gwyn or anyone else that she had neglected to inform her baby's father that she was pregnant. No one had said a word about it, no one had remarked his sudden absence, but within a half hour they had all gone home, all but Gwyn and her two kids, who were even now entertaining the girls and cleaning up after the party. The girls, fortunately, were completely absorbed in going through and dividing up the birthday gifts, much too happily occupied to pay attention to anything going on with the adults.

Backing out of the garage, Sierra tried to think where to begin looking. She decided to check the fields first. An hour passed before she could be reasonably certain that Sam was not out on one of his beloved tractors turning up the soil somewhere. The sun had set, the gloom quickly morphing into a night too soft for all the sharp fear and regret knifing through it.

She turned her car toward his place, thinking that her only other reasonable option would be the Houstons. When she pulled into his yard some minutes later, she felt a great relief that she would not have to face his foster parents with the ugly truth. That relief did not lessen the dread with which she contemplated facing Sam himself.

Working up her courage required several moments, but she told herself that she deserved whatever condemnation Sam would deliver. What mattered most, however, was that Sam did not deserve what she had done to him and that she'd do everything in her power to make it right. Resolved, she got out of the car and walked to the house on trembling legs.

He answered her knock within moments. His face bland, his manner relaxed, he nodded as if he'd been expecting her and stepped aside. "Come in."

She ducked her head, shoved her hands into the pockets of her corduroy jacket and entered the small, sparse living room. A cardboard box filled with framed photos rested on the seat of the couch. She glanced around the room, noting the bare spots on the wall.

"Not much to look at," he commented lightly.

"It doesn't matter. It never mattered."

"I know, but it's all the inheritance that my mother left my sisters and me, that and the horror of her death. I always wanted the twins to have more."

"You've given them more, Sam."

He nodded, seeming to accept that. "And there's more to come," he said. "I'm going to tear down this old house, and plant the ground with flowers. Don't know why I didn't think of it before."

Sierra looked around her once more, and her gaze went again to that box. She knew what he was planning, and she couldn't let him do it. "You can't move in with me, Sam."

"No?" he said lightly. "Well, you and Tyree sure can't move in here."

Sweet Sam, she thought, fresh tears gathering in her eyes. True to form, he had already accepted his fate and faced his responsibilities. "No one's moving anywhere, at least not right away."

He brought his hands to his hips. "Want to explain that?"

She turned away from him, hugging herself. "Nothing to explain. I just don't think it's wise."

"Wise?" he echoed. "When have we ever done what was wise? The wise thing would have been to keep our relationship strictly business, but we both know that was never even an option."

She bowed her head. "I'm so sorry, Sam. I can't tell you how sorry I am. This is all my fault."

"Sierra," he began, but she held up a hand to stop him, plunging on before she lost her nerve.

"I wish I could tell you that the baby was an accident, but I can't. I realized after the first time that I could be pregnant, and I knew even then that you would never walk away from your responsibilities the way Dennis did and always will. I—I suggested the condoms, but I didn't tell you why." She took a deep breath and tried to control the quiver in her voice. "And then I just let it go. I told myself that it was too late anyway, that I had raised one child on my own and could do it again. I'm certainly better able to afford it. But that's not why I did it, Sam."

"I know that," he said softly.

She covered her face with her hands so that he wouldn't have to see the teardrops rolling down her cheeks. "I meant to trap you, Sam. Deep down, I wanted you so badly that I was willing to trap you.'' She lifted her face to him, dashing away the tears, imploring him with her eyes. ''But the joke's on me, because I love you too much to do that to you.''

''I know that, too,'' he said.

She felt a whisper of relief. ''You do?''

He nodded and lifted both hands to her forearms. ''I've known for a long time. It was obvious.''

The feel of his hands swept through her in a warm, bittersweet rush. She closed her eyes. ''Then you must understand why I can't let you settle for anything less than what I feel for you.''

''Yes.''

That single word felt like a knife in her heart. She tried to breathe around the pain and couldn't quite manage. ''Then you agree that our relationship has to end here and now.''

He dropped his hands and backed up. ''What?''

''I'll find someone to buy me out.''

''Like hell.''

Her eyes popped open. ''O-okay. Uh, you can buy me out then. I should've realized you'd want to do that.''

''No one's buying anyone out,'' he stated flatly.

For a moment she thought he expected her to *give* him her share of the partnership, but then she realized that Sam would never do such a thing. If anything, he'd walk away and leave it with her. She shook her head. ''No. I can't let you abandon everything you've worked for.''

''Aban—'' He broke off and stared at her. His

hand came up, swept over his mouth, came to rest on his chin. "After all that's happened, you think I would abandon everything I've worked so hard for?"

She blinked at him. "I guess I don't understand what you want."

"Obviously!" He reached for her, shook her slightly. "What do you think I've been doing, Sierra? Why do you think I've broken my back to prove that I'm your equal?"

"You're more than my equal, Sam."

He stared down at her, searching her face. "You really don't get it, do you? I thought if it was obvious to me that it must be obvious to you. Don't you know how much I love you?"

A great and powerful joy washed over her, rocking her slightly, but she dared not trust it. "You don't have to say that."

He closed his eyes and let his head drop. "Evidently I should have said it a long time ago. I guess I didn't realize how important the words were." He opened his eyes and looked at her imploringly. "I almost told you a couple times, but somehow I didn't get it out. I can't believe you didn't know. I—I guess I was waiting for a perfect moment, and…every moment with you is perfect. I love you, honey. I'm sorry I didn't tell you before."

This time the wave knocked her off her feet. She swayed, knees buckling, but he caught her and locked her tight against him.

"Sierra? Honey?" He hustled her toward the couch, half dragging, half carrying. Plopping down, he pulled her onto his lap. "You okay?" His hand went to protectively to her belly.

She couldn't answer him with anything more than a nod before the tears came again. He pulled her head down onto his shoulder.

"Aw, sweetheart, don't cry." He pressed his hand to her cheek, ducked his chin and began kissing her. "It's okay."

"You love me?" she squeaked, lifting her head.

He nodded, smoothing her hair, then cupped her face with his hands. "You're the very center of my life, Sierra. You're the linchpin. Because of you, I have everything I've ever wanted." He dropped his hand to her belly again, massaging gently. "Or soon will." He gave her a lopsided grin. "My only problem now is how to explain that to Tyree."

Sierra laughed. "You'll find a way. You always do."

"So you'll marry me then?"

She grasped the wrist of the hand that still cupped her cheek. "Oh, Sam. Are you sure?"

"I won't take no for an answer. I mean it, Sierra. Baby or no baby."

She wrapped her arms around him, bursting with happiness. "Is tomorrow soon enough?"

He put his head back and sighed, a sound deep with relief and satisfaction. She kissed him, pressing her mouth down on his. Shifting, he laid her back in his arms until the box he'd been packing blocked them. His tongue plunged into her mouth, urgent and possessive. Desire flamed, rose, raged. He slid an arm beneath her knees and stood, the other arm supporting her back. She marveled at his strength.

"Where are we going?"

He smiled. "To make a baby."

She lifted an eyebrow. "Little late, isn't it?"

"We'll make it retroactively."

She thought she might burst with sheer joy. "Shouldn't we be planning a wedding first?"

He nodded, carrying her through the kitchen and into the bedroom. "I'm thinking simple and quick."

"Me, too."

"Not tomorrow, though, sweetheart. I have to see the lawyer tomorrow. The minute he can get that prenup drawn, we'll do it."

"No," she said.

He stopped next to the bed. "No?"

"No prenup, absolutely not."

He let her down, lowering her legs to the floor. "Sierra, you know how I feel about this."

"I will not sign a prenuptial agreement."

His eyebrows climbed, and he brought his hands to his hips. "Okay, never mind me, but what about Tyree? She needs to be protected. We need to set up a trust or—"

"No," she interrupted firmly, folding her arms.

"You don't want to protect your daughter's financial future?"

"We have four children," she said, holding up that many fingers.

"Almost," he qualified. "So far."

"And they will be treated equally. I mean it,

Sam, no matter how many children we wind up with. What's mine is yours and what's yours is mine, and that means that what *we* have, now and in the future, will be split equally among our heirs, all of them.''

He stared at her for a moment, then a smile began to grow across his face. That smile grew into a chuckle, and that chuckle swelled into laughter that doubled him over at the waist, hands on his knees.

At first Sierra was pleased, but then she grew concerned. "Sam? Sam?"

He straightened suddenly and threw out his arms. "Okay. You're right. You win. I had to get my pride out of the way to see it, but in the end I find that I have to bow to the superior wisdom of an older woman."

Sierra gasped, but then she smiled. "I'm going to remind you of that every day for the rest of your life."

He swept her into his arms and tumbled them both onto the bed. "I'm counting on it." Rolling her onto her back, he straddled her and began crawling out of his shirt, grinning as wide as the room. "I love you, Sierra," he said. "I love all my girls. I love this baby we're making and the life we're building and the farm we're growing and every moment I've spent with you since I first met you." He tossed the shirt and fell forward, bracing himself above her on his long, strong arms. "I love the way your hair curls and the way your eyes flash when your temper gets the better of you, and I love the way you catch your breath when I put myself inside you. I love the sex. Most of all, I love the way you love me.''

"Sam," she said, looking up into his face. "Sam." Happy tears rolled out of her eyes and into the hair at her temples. "Sam."

"Yeah," he said, bending his head to hers, "just like that."

She wrapped her arms around him, and as his clever hands and drugging mouth told her the truth behind the words he had given her, her mind spun back to the moment when she had learned what Edwin Searle had done for her and the others.

The shock of that moment, of hearing her name listed among those of Edwin's beneficiaries, hearing the incredible news that she had just become an instant millionaire, lived vividly in her memory. She couldn't have known then that Edwin's ultimate gift to her would be a love as certain and rich as his own had been. All those flowers that he had laid on his wife's cold grave had been more than a simple sign of his enduring devotion, they had been a promise, a down payment on the true inheritance he'd held in store for those lucky enough to find themselves beneficiaries of Edwin Searle's largesse.

What Edwin had left was not money but the opportunity to find true wealth, the kind of love that he himself had valued more than all his millions. Val had found it with Ian, a love so rich that they had simply decided to give away or set aside her wealth. Now, because she'd had the money to reach for her dreams, Sierra had found it with Sam, and as he proved to her one more time that he was the true answer to those dreams, she hoped with all her heart that Avis would be next.

Sierra finally understood just what it meant to be rich, and it wasn't about money. Money was nice, but love was everything.

Absolutely everything.

* * * * *

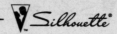

SPECIAL EDITION™

Three small-town women have their lives turned
upside down by a sudden inheritance.
Change is good, but change this big?

by Arlene James

BEAUTICIAN GETS MILLION-DOLLAR TIP!

(Silhouette Special Edition #1589,
available January 2004)

A sexy commitment-shy fire marshal meets his match
in a beautician with big...bucks?

FORTUNE FINDS FLORIST

(Silhouette Special Edition #1596,
available February 2004)

It's time to get down and dirty when a beautiful
florist teams up with a sexy farmer....

TYCOON MEETS TEXAN!

(Silhouette Special Edition #1601,
available March 2004)

The trip of a lifetime turns into something more
when a widow is swept off her feet by someone
tall, dark and wealthy....

Available at your favorite retail outlet.

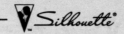

SPECIAL EDITION™

·MERLYN COUNTY·

MIDWIVES

Delivering the miracle of life…and love!

In March 2004, meet the newest arrival at Merlyn County Regional Hospital, in

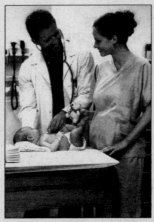

BLUEGRASS BABY
Judy Duarte
(Silhouette Special Edition #1598)

One night of heart-stealing passion with midwife Milla Johnson left Dr. Kyle Bingham wanting more—as long as he could have her without settling down. But what would he do once he learned Milla's precious secret? Could imminent fatherhood—and love—make a family man out of Merlyn County's most marriage-shy bachelor?

Don't miss the continuation of Merlyn County Midwives!

Forever…Again by Maureen Child
(Silhouette Special Edition #1604, available April 2004)

In the Enemy's Arms by Pamela Toth
(Silhouette Special Edition #1610, available May 2004)

Available at your favorite retail outlet.

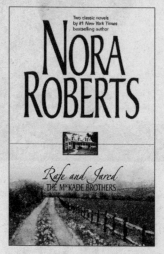

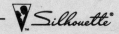

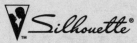

COMING NEXT MONTH